ALL THE BAD GIRLS

A Special Agent Lexi Stone Thriller

Kim Cresswell

KC Publishing

Cover Art © 2024 by RCSbookcovers
Published by KC Publishing

ISBN-978-1-990225-10-9

For Justin, Carla, Porter, Peyton, and Leo

In memory of Mary Beech

Death leaves a heartache no one can heal, love leaves a memory no one can steal.
— From a headstone in Ireland

CHAPTER ONE

*H*is heart pounded in his chest. Each beat echoed in his ears, drowning out the traffic speeding by. Grasping the rope tightly with both hands, he watched her from the far corner of the club. For days, he had observed her, tracking her with the patience of a predator waiting for the perfect moment to strike.

No turning back now.

As she headed to her car, he charged toward her, closing the gap with alarming speed.

She spun around, clutching her car keys, her emerald eyes huge with surprise and fear.

He grabbed her from behind, yanking her against his body. She tried to pull away and elbowed him in the ribs. He wrapped the rope around her neck until it dug into her flesh. She let out a stifled scream, her body thrashing against his.

Long manicured nails clawed at his black gloves, scratching at the thick leather, attempting to tear through the protective barrier. He felt the struggle leave her body and she exhaled one last breath. Once, her body was limp, he dragged her backward. The heels of her shoes scratched against the pavement. In a swift, brutal motion, he tossed her inside the pickup truck.

He slammed the door shut, sealing her fate, and hopped in on the driver's side. Staring at her vacant eyes, surprisingly, he felt nothing. A sense of righteousness filled him as he started the engine. Everything he had done, every life he had taken, was for Lexi.

CHAPTER TWO

Lexi's cell phone rang, shattering the fragile morning stillness with its piercing ringtone. She answered without checking the caller ID. "Agent Stone."

"I hope you've had your double-shot of caffeine."

Jake, her partner, was always the bearer of bad news. "What's up?"

"Just got a call. State law enforcement has requested the FBI's assistance, specifically us."

In the bathroom, Lexi switched the phone to speaker and hastily yanked her brown hair into a ponytail. "What are we facing?"

"Three bodies in Boardman Lake."

Her heart stuttered at the news. She knew the area well from childhood summers spent swimming and camping there. They were about to be drawn into a major investigation, and she braced herself for what might be waiting for them at the crime scene.

"Possible serial killer." The words hung heavy in the air. "I'll meet you there," Jake said at last.

Lexi tried to ignore the mounting stress. In less than eight weeks, she would be walking down the aisle. The amount of work left on the to-do list was overwhelming. She quickly pulled on a white shirt and navy tactical slacks. "I'm on my way."

Cracking a case like this was every agent's dream. Lexi had devoted the past decade to the Traverse City FBI, tackling violent crimes, hunting down serial murderers, and working on special jurisdictional homicides. She and Jake were an elite duo, two of a small percentage of agents who specialized in serial murders. Lexi didn't want to think about the backlog of paperwork stacked on her desk or how her plans for the day had just been tossed out the window. They would be under immense pressure to apprehend the killer before he struck again.

With her extensive training at the FBI Academy, a master's in forensic psychology, and her natural talent for profiling and reading body language, she was born to hunt down bad guys. It was her calling, in her DNA, passed down from her father, a retired agent. If they were dealing with a serial killer, she would find him and bring him to justice.

The aroma of freshly brewed coffee led her to the kitchen to find Adam in a white t-shirt and gray sweatpants, cooking bacon and eggs. This was their only time together, the weekends, the rare moments when their worlds intertwined. Service always came with a cost. Guilt twisted her throat at the thought of disappointing him again. He was a good guy, kind and loyal. A real catch, her mother often said. It was one of the few things they agreed on.

Lexi stared at the wedding planner's binder spread across the dining table, each page filled with vibrant flower arrangements and elegant table settings. "I have to go," she said, trying to hide her disappointment.

"I figured." Adam wiped his hands on a towel. "Guess I better reschedule with the wedding planner."

"I'm sorry."

"We'll make it work."

They were getting married in January and were supposed to scout out potential wedding venues after lunch. This wasn't the first time they'd had to postpone. It was the fourth and probably not the last.

"We've still got plenty of time," he said and handed her a thermos of black coffee. "I'd marry you anywhere, anytime. We can always do city hall as a last resort."

She managed a smile, grateful for his support, and put on her coat. "At this rate, we might have to."

Tall and broad-shouldered, Adam Quinn was the opposite of her ex-husband, Nick Brody, a detective with the Sheriff's Department's major crimes division, in every way possible. As a senior reporter with the Traverse City Record, Adam knew all too well how his job could wreak havoc with their personal lives. Add her job to the mix, and it was a potential recipe for disaster. Between their crazy schedules, long hours, and Adam's intense deadlines, they still had something special, and nothing was going to ruin their relationship.

They had met two years ago during one of the numerous media encounters in the press room at the FBI office, and it was love at first sight. Easygoing and kind, Adam never pressured her. He was exactly what she needed—the one person she could always trust.

As if on cue, his cell phone vibrated and danced across the marble countertop. He checked the text message, and his blue eyes met hers. "Three bodies. This doesn't sound good."

Lexi looped her FBI credentials around her neck. Unease crept up her spine. "It's going to be a long day for both of us."

Even though he usually received his tips covertly through the county sheriff's department, the news of a possible serial killer would spread rapidly, causing panic and fear.

He wrapped his arms around her waist and drew her close. "How about Chinese take-out for a late-night dinner?"

Lexi savored the warmth of his embrace and felt the affection he had for her. Knowing they wouldn't have much of a social life in the foreseeable future, she wanted to spend as much time with him as she could. "Sounds perfect. And don't forget the wine."

"You can count on it." He kissed her forehead. "Be careful out there."

"Always," Lexi said and headed out the door.

#

The area around the lake was vibrant with trees, their leaves blazing shades of amber, gold, and red. It had been unseasonably mild for November, with daytime highs in the mid-fifties, which was a good thing. Otherwise, the lake would have been frozen over, and the bodies wouldn't have been discovered until spring. When she pulled up to the scene, emergency vehicles lined the shoulder of the road leading into the area. Unmarked units with lights flashing filed one by one into a makeshift parking lot. Yellow police tape flapped in the wind. A large number of law enforcement officers gathered outside their vehicles, chatting.

Lexi parked behind one of the sheriff department's cruisers and killed the engine. She opened the door and paused before getting out. Cool air filled her lungs. A news helicopter circled overhead, its presence a reminder of the potential chaos that could spiral out of control. After she showed her credentials to a young male officer, he lifted the police tape, and she ducked underneath. Jake met her a few yards in. He was four inches taller than her at five-foot-eleven with a rock-solid build, and his clean-shaven face possessed a boyish charm.

"Not exactly how you pictured your Saturday," he said and flashed a tight smile.

"No one wants to spend the weekend like this. We had to cancel with the wedding planner again."

"Maybe it's a sign. I mean, you're already living together. Does a piece of paper really make much difference now?"

Lexi ignored his comment and changed the subject. "What are we looking at?"

"Three females in their twenties. I wanted to wait for you so we could go over the scene together."

"Who was the first to arrive?" Lexi asked.

He jerked a thumb over his shoulder in the direction of a female patrol officer with stylish short black hair. "She secured the immediate perimeter until backup arrived. Two kayakers discovered the bodies and called it in. The local cops are interviewing them right now."

Sunlight glistened on the surface of the water, and Lexi squinted against the glare. Three hundred and seventeen acres with multiple docks and hiking trails. Securing it all would be a challenge. Not to mention someone would have to sift through an enormous number of hours of CCTV footage to identify every vehicle's plate that had entered the area. She glanced at the dark gray clouds in the distance, rolling in from the east. The scene needed to be processed immediately in case it rained, or they could lose crucial evidence.

"Isn't this a pleasant surprise?" a deep voice said from behind her.

Lexi's mouth went dry. She was hoping not to run into her ex-husband. No such luck. They hadn't worked on a case together since before the divorce over four years ago. Boundaries were never his strong suit. Nick truly believed she would come back to him after he'd had an affair with a young school liaison officer.

Tension gripped her shoulders, and she turned to face him. "Hello, Nick."

"Hey, good to see you."

Standing five-foot-nine, Nick had a strong jawline

and piercing blue eyes which at times looked right through you. His short blond hair was always slicked back with obsessive attention, and today was no exception.

He held her gaze for a long moment, then his brows came together. "These murders have serial killer written all over them."

"Who's running lead?" Jake asked.

Lexi inwardly groaned, already knowing the answer. She fiddled with her coat's zipper, trying to suppress her frustration at having to work with him.

Nick puffed out his chest. "You're looking at him."

She still hadn't come to terms with the fact she had made a colossal mistake marrying him and probably never would. Even her mother had tried to warn her, but she had been too blind to see the truth.

As she walked a few steps behind Nick, reporters and news vehicles fought for a front-row seat on the other side of the heavy-duty plastic barricade. The growing flurry of activity was always about which news outlet could break the story first. The competition for information turned red-hot, and Lexi spotted Adam speaking with a member of the K-9 unit. The sight of him grounded her and calmed her nerves.

Nick pulled on a pair of latex gloves and frowned. "The third body has just been recovered from the lake. Be warned. It ain't pretty."

Lexi braced herself for the worst.

While making their way down an embankment

leading to the lake, every nerve ending was telling her this was just the beginning for the killer. The FBI's Evidence Response Team, composed of highly trained and skilled forensic examiners, technicians, and agents, collected evidence and took photographs. Another tech placed yellow evidence markers next to one of the docks. A black drone buzzed past her, collecting video footage of the area. Inhaling a deep breath, she steeled herself and pulled out a pair of latex gloves from her jacket pocket. Lexi put them on, and Jake followed her lead.

"Is the ME here?" she asked.

Nick shook his head. "He should be here any minute." He hesitated, then pulled back a white sheet covering one of the bodies. "Meet Jane Doe Number 1."

Lexi heard her own sharp intake of breath.

Jake's jaw dropped. "Jesus Christ. What's up with the wooden cross?"

He took the words right out of her mouth. Insects had already begun feasting on the dead woman's flesh. Flies swarmed around her, and she batted them away. Acidic bile rose at the back of her throat. She swallowed hard and tried to make sense of what was in front of her. "Why tether her to a wooden cross? Torture? Religious reasons?"

Jake shrugged. "Any way you look at it, it's messed up. Birds pecked out her eyeballs. They're gone."

Her instincts kicked in again. "The killer isn't done. Expect more bodies."

Nick glanced at her, and his eyes told her he

was worried too that more victims would turn up. "Aren't you full of good news? Hope you're wrong. We have to find this sick bastard."

Lexi knelt in front of the naked body. Long blonde hair fanned out across bony shoulders. She pointed to the woman's swollen and bruised neck. "Notice the edema, lacerations, and abrasions? That's a ligature mark. She was strangled, probably with the same rope used to bind her wrists and ankles to the cross." She looked up at Nick. "Are they all like this?"

He nodded. "And get this. The crosses all have flotation devices attached to them. The bodies were meant to stay afloat."

Jake shook his head. "That's fucked up."

"The killer revels in displaying his work." Lexi stood. In her thirty-five years, she had never witnessed anything of this magnitude. She noted the scratch marks on the woman's neck and the five broken, pink-painted fingernails. The woman had fought fiercely against her attacker. She took out her cell phone and snapped a couple of pictures, focusing on the woman's injuries.

"We'll know more once the autopsies are done." Nick covered up the body, his gaze landing on hers. "Let's grab a drink and discuss the use of the wooden crosses."

It was always all about him. His invitation was personal, and under the circumstances, she had no patience for his games. "No thanks on the drink."

"Come on. It won't hurt. I promise. You used to enjoy a good bottle of wine." He cracked a small grin, his boyish charm severely misplaced in the current situation.

She knew his behavior would only worsen if she didn't stop it. Squaring her shoulders, Lexi spoke firmly so he would get the message. "Let's keep this on a professional level. You're more than welcome to visit the FBI office to discuss the case."

Nick stripped off his gloves and pocketed them with a sense of finality. "I have to speak with the sheriff and bring him up to speed. I'll catch up with you two later. Keep me updated." He turned and walked away in the opposite direction.

Jake shook his head. "I can't believe he's still pursuing you after all these years."

"I can't believe I married him."

"Do you want me to talk to him?" Jake offered.

Having grown up with an alcoholic mother, Lexi had learned to fend for herself. "I'll handle it. Right now, we have a killer to find."

#

Lexi trudged back up the sandy embankment when her cell phone rang. She yanked it out of her pocket, swiped a finger over the touch screen, and hit the speaker icon. "Agent Stone."

"Did you hear about the bodies at the lake? I can't believe it."

"Mom, I'm in the middle of something right now""

Her mother's voice boomed through the phone's speaker. "It's terrible. I hope they catch the killer."

"I have to go," Lexi said.

"Are you and Adam still coming for dinner

tonight?"

"Not tonight. We'll catch up when things calm down a bit at work."

A long pause followed on the other end. "Okay, I have to go. Your father's ready to leave for errands."

The call ended abruptly, leaving Lexi's eyes glued to her phone. Her mother's fifteen years of sobriety, though hard-won, did little to ease the pain of a childhood she spent in neglect. The teenage years had been the worst, the shame and isolation staying with her into adulthood. Even now, Lexi often daydreamed about a different childhood. With a determined shake of her head, she forced herself to focus on the present.

While Jake spoke with one of the crime scene techs, she thought about the victims. The women were so young, their lives tragically cut short. It was a sad situation. Walking to her SUV, she spotted Adam approaching, his smile a welcome sight. At six-foot-one and ruggedly handsome, he was surprisingly composed, despite the pressure he would be facing to get this story out. Her gaze roamed over his face.

"How are you holding up?" he asked, running a hand through his wavy hair.

"I've seen better days."

"I bet. We can discuss it at home if you want."

"Definitely. I need to start working on a profile to understand what we're up against."

"Any leads on the victims' identities?"

"Not yet."

"Do we have a serial killer on the loose in Traverse City?"

Lexi locked eyes with him. "Off the record?"

He nodded.

"It appears that way."

"Sounds like a bloody nightmare." A heavy silence hung between them. "I was surprised to see Nick Brody."

"Believe me, it was a surprise to me too. Unfortunately, he's in charge of this one."

He arched an eyebrow, his gaze probing hers. "Do you think it's a coincidence you're involved?"

Her palms grew clammy. Lexi desperately wanted to believe her ex-husband had brought her and Jake in for their expertise, but she wasn't convinced. "Nothing Nick does is ever a coincidence."

"You know, if he keeps bothering you, something has to be done."

Adam wasn't the jealous type. His concern was genuine. Things had spiraled out of control. For the past four years, Nick had contacted her, showed up uninvited to their house, and even sent flowers to her just last week. The man needed to leave her alone and accept she had moved on.

"Let's discuss it later," she said, determined to focus on the case and not let anything, especially her ex-husband, distract her.

"Just be careful. I don't trust him."

"Don't worry. I've got it under control." Lexi let her gaze shift to Jake walking toward them.

The two men barely acknowledged each other.

"I'll text you later." Adam kissed her on the cheek then walked back in the direction of the barricade.

"Was it something I said?" Jake asked.

Lexi wasn't sure how to respond. "He's on a tight deadline. You know what it's like."

The relationship between Adam and Jake had always piqued her curiosity. Despite growing up in Ohio, playing football together, attending the same high school and college, and finding themselves working in Traverse City, they weren't friends. It was a weird situation, a mystery. Neither man was willing to talk about it.

"The K-9 unit found a white sock, pink running shoe, and a silver charm bracelet," Jake said. "It's unclear if they belong to any of the victims."

"We'll find out soon enough," Lexi said, pushing a loose strand of hair away from her face. "The killer wanted the bodies to be found."

"The flotation devices are a real sick touch. I'll start running background checks on the kayakers. Do you think our guy is selecting specific victims or trying to send a message?"

The last thing she wanted to do was fall into a tunnel vision trap. It happened all too often in cases like this. "It's too early to tell, but I'd say he definitely sent a message. He wanted us to see what he's capable of."

"I'll check for CCTV footage in the area and meet you back at the office," Jake said.

After he left, Lexi was relieved to see the medical examiner, a slim man with thick black hair who walked with a slight limp. She made her way over to him and introduced herself. "Hi. I'm FBI Agent Lexi Stone."

"Nice to meet you." He shook her hand but didn't smile. "Michael Chen." His brown eyes shifted to the credentials hanging around her neck. "This isn't something you see every day."

"You're telling me. It's pretty twisted."

"All three victims were likely strangled with a rope or cord, indicating the same killer. They were killed elsewhere."

Lexi sighed. "That means there are three other crime scenes out there."

"Unfortunately."

"Do you think the deaths were premeditated or spontaneous?"

"The injuries suggest the perpetrator took his time, ensuring the victims were dead before disposing of their bodies. It was cold and calculated. Time of death estimates align within a day or two of each other."

"The possible religious or ritualistic motive is intriguing," Lexi said, thinking out loud. "I don't think the killer is finished."

"Exactly my thoughts. Let's hope we're both wrong."

She handed him one of her cards. "Let me know when you have an ID on the women."

The sun vanished during her walk back to her SUV, and she quickened her pace. Fat raindrops splattered against her coat, mirroring the intensity of the crime scene. Three young women weren't returning home. Whoever had committed the murders had been methodical. Lexi had to find him. She couldn't let the families down. Failure was not an option.

#

Inside the bustling FBI building, Lexi maneuvered through the crowd, past the metal detectors, and took the elevator to the third floor. Quiet conversations, phones blaring, and the clatter of keyboards filled the air. Cubicles occupied by agents formed a grid-like pattern, their faces reflecting on their computer screens. She found Jake in the main conference room examining the drone footage he had set up on a large monitor.

"Find anything interesting?" She took off her coat and tossed it on a chair.

"Absolutely nothing."

She eyed the whiteboard and corkboard covered in crime scene photos, victim close-ups, photos of the wooden crosses, a map of the lake, and other case-related material. "These murders are part of a larger scheme. We just haven't figured out his motive yet. The perpetrator is highly organized."

"Why dump them at the lake?" Jake asked.

"Perhaps something traumatic occurred there. Something he can't let go of."

His gaze met hers, and he massaged his temples. "At this point, we've got no leads. What's the plan?"

Taking a seat, she opened her laptop. "The usual. Establish connections between the victims as soon as we know who they are: relationships, shared experiences, anything linking them together. I'll work on constructing the killer's profile." Lexi crafted detailed profiles for each victim using the crime scene information and victimology that she had. When she finished fifteen minutes later, she printed a copy of the profile and placed it on the scarred tabletop. "I'm not completely convinced the crosses hold a religious significance. I think they're a message, a display of his power."

Leaning back, Jake interlocked his hands behind his neck. "Might be. Maybe he sees himself as judge and jury and used the crosses as a means of punishment."

Lexi went to the window and considered the idea. She turned. "The killer might believe the victims violated some moral or biblical code. Did the background checks on the kayakers turn up anything?"

He shook his head. "Not even a parking ticket. They were in the wrong place at the wrong time."

She refused to dismiss any possibilities this early in the investigation. Glancing at her watch, she closed the laptop. "We have a briefing with Williams in a few minutes. I almost forgot."

"Can't wait," Jake said, his voice dripping with sarcasm. "You know how he gets when he doesn't feel an investigation is moving along fast enough."

David Williams, their SAC, was a man with a quick temper who at times lacked social finesse. They had worked together on a case six years ago. An eight-year-old boy kidnapped from his school playground, held for ransom. His father, Lucas Turner, a billionaire tech tycoon. The child never made it home. He was found at East Bay Park in one of the picnic areas. It was a case that haunted Lexi to this day.

"He can be a special kind of asshole," Jake muttered, standing up. He took a step toward the door.

Lexi laughed and grabbed the profile from the conference table. "We aren't rushing this investigation, regardless of what he says."

Jake nodded and followed her to the end of the corridor to the briefing room.

When they walked in, their SAC, a forgettable-looking man in his fifties with a shrinking hairline, was sitting at the head of the table, reading a file. His head snapped up, his expression somber, and he gestured for them to sit. Behind him, a large map of the city hung on the wall. Lexi and Jake took a seat across from each other.

"Got a profile?" Williams asked, getting straight to the point.

She nodded and read from the printout. "The offender is believed to be a white male between the ages of twenty-five and forty. He's intelligent and well-educated. He possesses a fascination with power and control, paired with a startling absence of empathy and a willingness to harm others for his own benefit. His adeptness at eluding discovery reveals a methodical, calculated approach to both committing and concealing his crimes. A traumatic event from his past probably triggered his descent into violence, creating a disconnect from empathy and remorse. He may have a history of violence against women. The victims were killed elsewhere and transported to the lake, suggesting a familiarity with the area or personal significance to him. He also exhibits strong organizational skills and knowledge of forensic techniques." Handing him the profile, she added, "That pretty much sums it up. I'll update it once we have the medical examiner's report. We're also exploring a possible religious connection due to the use of wooden crosses. It's not something we can rule out at this point."

"Obviously, we're dealing with a real sick individual. Any suspects?"

Lexi shook her head.

His expression remained unchanged. "The public is in a state of panic, and the media is pushing hard for answers we don't have. They've dubbed him the 'Lakeside Killer.' We need results quickly."

She cringed, anticipating the media storm they would have to navigate.

"We'll get the profile circulated." Williams fixed her with a long look. "Detective Brody is in charge. All information flows through him and this office. No comments to the media other than the investigation is ongoing."

"Understood," Lexi said, meeting his gaze.

"Considering your previous relationship with Brody, I trust you can work together again without any issues."

Lexi clenched her teeth, resenting the insinuation, but refrained from responding, fearing it would worsen things. Instead, she nodded.

He stood abruptly and his expression grew serious again. "You'll have all the necessary resources at your disposal. We can't afford any mistakes on this one. Be prepared for long hours until the perpetrator is apprehended. You know how this works. I expect daily updates."

The pressure was on. Sleep would be a luxury.

"That was fun," Jake said, rolling his eyes.

"You're right. He's an uptight piece of work," she said over her shoulder. Her cell phone buzzed, and Lexi quickly answered. "Agent Stone."

"I've got something for you."

She couldn't help rolling her eyes. "Nick, what is it?"

"The lab completed the analysis of the bracelet found at the scene. They found a fingerprint. It matches a guy by the name of Carl Jefferson Blunt, forty-four. He has a history of violence against women."

Goosebumps prickled her skin. This could be their guy. "Where is he now?"

"We picked him up ten minutes ago."

"We're leaving now," Lexi said, ending the call.

CHAPTER THREE

Arriving at the Sheriff's Department, Lexi and Jake were met by a swarm of reporters vying for a statement. Pushing through the crowd, they made their way inside the building to one of the interrogation rooms.

The space was windowless, suffocatingly cramped, with a scratched metal table along one wall and two chairs that had seen better days. Carl Blunt sat handcuffed to a shackling iron welded to the table, wearing a two-tone blue plaid shirt and blue jeans. His salt and pepper hair was unkempt and in desperate need of a trim. Jake and Nick moved to opposite sides of the room to put space between them.

"Why is he cuffed?" Lexi asked.

"The bastard tried to run," Nick said, visibly seething, judging by the way a vein in his neck was bulging. "He thinks he's above the law."

Blunt shot him a venomous glare. "That's a lie. You saw my record and jumped to conclusions. No wonder nobody trusts the cops anymore."

Lexi took a seat across from the man. "Carl, I'm Special Agent Lexi Stone with the FBI. I'd like to ask you a few questions."

"What's this all about? I got nothing to hide," he said, maintaining eye contact.

She needed to establish trust immediately, or the interview would end prematurely. Lexi glanced at Nick. "Remove the cuffs."

Nick's hands balled into fists, but he complied.

Blunt rubbed his wrists, and his one leg twitched. "He's full of shit. I never tried to run."

"I believe you," she said calmly, redirecting his attention to her.

His bushy eyebrows arched. "You do?"

She nodded. "Were you informed about why we wanted to speak with you?"

His eyes settled on Nick with renewed anger. "He said I hurt some women. I sure-as-hell didn't. I turned my life around five years ago. Quit drinking. Been clean ever since. My record says so." He stared hard and pointed at Nick. "Then he started roughing me up."

Lexi believed the part about the rough treatment. She had witnessed Nick's aggressive behavior before. It was as if he couldn't turn off the adrenaline rush once it began. "We found one of your fingerprints on a silver bracelet at Boardman Lake." Sliding a photograph of the jewelry across the table, she waited for his reaction.

Confusion clouded his face. "That's—that's my daughter Emma's bracelet."

Sitting up straight, Lexi's interest intensified. "When was she last at the lake?"

Carl exhaled heavily, shrugging. "I have no idea.

Has something happened to her?"

She waited a beat. "Why would you ask that?"

"Because you wouldn't have dragged me in over a bracelet." After a brief pause, he hesitated. "Is Emma okay?"

She couldn't provide an answer or dismiss the possibility his daughter was among the victims. Shifting her line of questioning, she tried to reassure him. "We just want to make sure Emma is safe. When did you last see or speak with her?"

"Thursday, on her birthday. That's when I gave her the bracelet. Her car broke down and she needed a ride to work. She's a waitress at the Crave Haven Club."

Lexi wrote it down on the notepad in front of her and circled it. She was familiar with the club, a popular spot with the younger crowd, featuring electronic music and live performances. "What time was that?"

"Around four o'clock. Her shift started at four-thirty, and she was worried about being late. Her boss is kind of an A-hole."

"Have you spoken with her since?"

He shook his head. "It's not like her to not check in."

"Did she seem upset or worried on Thursday?"

"Not at all. She was happy, like any other day other than her car breaking down."

"Is there anyone who might want to harm her?"

"No. Everyone loves Emma. I raised her on my own after her mother passed away when she was fifteen," Carl said, his voice breaking. "She planned on moving out and getting her own place when she could afford it."

"Was there anyone new in her life? A boyfriend?"

Several beats of painful silence hung in the air.

"She didn't have time for one. Emma was focused on work and her part-time nursing studies."

"Where did she study?"

"Northwestern."

Lexi exchanged a glance with Jake. The campus was situated five minutes away from the lake and raised the possibility all the victims were students. It was a new angle they needed to explore.

Carl's eyes welled up with tears. "She never came home from work that night. I've been trying to reach her ever since. She's not answering her phone. I've called the club. No one has seen her."

"My partner is going to accompany you downstairs to collect a DNA sample. We want to make sure nothing has happened to Emma, since she hasn't been in contact with you. Is that okay?"

Staring at her, he wiped his eyes with the back of his hand and nodded slowly.

Lexi walked him to the door and handed him her card. "I'll be in contact."

After Carl left the room with Jake, Nick paused at the door. "Do you believe him?"

Lexi debated discussing Nick's behavior, but now wasn't the time. The case took precedence. "He's telling the truth. His responses showed genuine concern. He's really worried about his daughter."

"I'm pretty sure he described one of the other victims."

Lexi felt a surge of empathy for the father. She couldn't imagine what it would be like to lose a child.

Nick headed to the door and retrieved his cellphone from his coat pocket. "I'll call the lab and expedite the DNA analysis."

#

By 3 PM, Lexi had polished off her fourth cup of coffee and sent the cup flying into the trashcan next to the desk. "What about the lake's CCTV footage?" she asked Jake.

He shrugged. "It's gone, kaput. Budget cuts."

Nothing surprised her anymore. Cuts, layoffs, broken systems. It was all too familiar.

"The cops are searching for security footage from nearby homes and businesses. Do you think Blunt's innocent?"

"I'd put money on it. The killer probably dropped the bracelet without realizing."

Jake shot her a sidelong glance, his attention divided between her and his laptop screen. "He might have wanted it as a souvenir."

"More than likely. It's a twisted way for him to relive the thrill, dehumanize his victims, and justify his actions." Just then, her cell phone rang. "Agent Stone."

"It's Michael Chen with the medical examiner's office. The lab results are in."

She straightened. "And?"

"As you suspected, the DNA matches one of the victims. Emma Blunt."

Sadness tugged at Lexi's heart. "What about the others and the sock and shoe found at the scene?"

"No results yet. I'll update you soon. Oh, and Agent Stone—"

"Please, call me Lexi."

"Regarding Emma, there weren't any signs of sexual assault."

"That's good to know."

"I'll prioritize the others for tomorrow morning."

"Thanks." She hung up and locked eyes with Jake. "It's her. Emma Blunt. She's one of the victims."

"I was hoping she had just run off with friends or something."

Lexi let out a breath. "Me too."

"The killer is sloppy. He left evidence behind," Jake said, his tone measured and serious.

"It could have been his first kill." Worry crept into her words. "When he realizes his mistake, he might strike again out of anger."

"We still have to search Blunt's property. If he is innocent like you believe, he has nothing to worry about."

Informing the grieving father about his daughter's death and handing him a search warrant gave her a stomachache. "Nothing like making a terrible situation worse."

Her phone vibrated with a text from Adam telling her he loved her and was looking forward to some time together later. The message warmed her heart. She smiled to herself, thankful for the interruption, and sent him back a message.

Can't wait. XOX

Jake passed her a piece of paper with Carl Blunt's address written on it.

She dialed Nick and felt her shoulders tensing, each second heightening her anxiety.

"Detective Brody," Nick said on the other end in his usual gruff voice.

"We're going to need a search warrant." Lexi briefed him on the situation.

"You have sufficient probable cause. I know you. Don't beat yourself up over this. You're doing your job."

Serving a warrant was never easy, and it was even more emotionally taxing when it involved a grieving father who had just lost his only child.

"I'll gather a team and meet you at Blunt's house in an hour with the warrant."

#

The home with faded green paint appeared out of place with the surrounding neighborhood's well-kept homes. Behind the small bungalow, an auto repair shop sat amidst a clutter of a half-dozen cars in various states of disrepair. Lexi parked the SUV behind an aging Ford F-150 pickup truck in the driveway. She unbuckled her seatbelt and hopped out. Gravel crunched under her boots. Nick and Jake were deep in conversation with members of the Evidence Response Team. They looked up as she approached.

"Jake has the warrant," Nick said. "I'll stay out here."

Lexi nodded, mindful of the tension between the two men. "Good choice, given the circumstances." Bracing herself, she strode to the front door and knocked.

Carl Blunt opened the door, and Lexi's throat constricted with emotion.

"Did you find Emma?" His voice trembled with hope and fear.

"We need to speak with you," she said gently. "Can we come in and talk?"

He hesitated, then stepped aside, allowing her and Jake to enter.

Inside, the living room was cramped with furniture, its beige walls and scuffed floors bearing the weight of time. An oversized gray recliner faced a big-screen TV, which Carl promptly turned off. Lexi's gaze swept the room, taking in the Bible on the coffee table and the family photos on one wall. She knew what she had to do. There was no point in sugar coating it. "I'm sorry to have to tell you this, but Emma is one of the victims found out at Boardman Lake."

Carl's face drained of color. "Are you sure it's Emma?"

Lexi nodded. "I'm sorry for your loss."

A long, painful silence followed.

"How was she killed?" Tears flooded the corners of his eyes. "Did she suffer?"

"We're waiting for confirmation from the

medical examiner as to the cause of death. Carl, she didn't suffer." Lexi hated deceiving him. The truth wouldn't bring his daughter back. It wouldn't change a damn thing. It would only deepen his pain.

"I don't understand. She was a good kid, never hurt anybody. I want to see her."

"You can, once the medical examiner is finished." After giving him a moment to compose himself, she continued, her voice gentle yet resolute. "We have to search your house and the auto repair shop."

Jake handed him the warrant, and the room fell silent once more.

Carl's face turned bright red. "Have you lost your fucking mind? You think I did this? I would never hurt my daughter."

She understood his reaction under the circumstances. "It's just a formality," she said, trying to calm him down. "We have to fully investigate her death. I'm sure you understand."

"I'll inform the team they can begin," Jake murmured, barely audible.

Lexi glanced at him. "Give us a few minutes. Tell them to start in the shop."

Jake left, and Carl sank into the recliner, clutching a framed photograph of his daughter. Emma's bright smile stared back at her. She swallowed hard, feeling his loss.

He looked up, his face filled with pain and shock. "How could this have happened? She just turned twenty-two."

"That's what we're going to find out." Lexi refocused her attention, needing to learn more. "Have you noticed any strange or unfamiliar vehicles near the property lately?"

He shook his head. "The people I deal with always call ahead and make an appointment."

"Does anyone else have access to the house or shop other than you and Emma?"

"No. We're the only ones with keys."

"You mentioned that Emma still lives at home. Could I see her room?" Lexi asked. "It might help with our investigation."

Reality settled in, and Carl slumped further in the chair. He pointed to the hallway.

She stopped and put her hand on his shoulder, then pulled a pair of latex gloves from her coat pocket and put them on. Making her way down the narrow hallway, she noticed a door ajar, revealing what appeared to be Carl's dark and cluttered bedroom.

Emma's room was bright and tidy. Fluffy white throw pillows were on the bed, and modern wall art frames added character. Her gaze moved to the desk, where a few open books lay next to a laptop. Lexi noted they were nursing textbooks. Trinkets, jewelry and cosmetics were neatly organized on the dresser beside a photograph of Emma and her father. Lexi picked up the photograph, a snapshot from Emma's high-school graduation. She had to admit the two looked happy. Voices from the living room grew louder, interrupting her thoughts.

Jake appeared in the doorway. "A couple of techs just walked in the house."

She put the photograph back on the dresser. "Did they find anything yet in the shop?"

"Nothing so far pointing to Blunt as the killer."

"I'm not surprised. Make sure Emma's laptop gets logged in. We need to know what's on it."

When they left the room and joined the team, Lexi glanced at Carl still in the recliner, staring off into space. She didn't have the heart to make him leave while the search was underway.

As they combed through the house, her mind raced. What happened to Emma and the other women? Did they know their killer? While the crime scene techs collected evidence and documented their findings, Lexi's determination to uncover the truth grew stronger.

Three hours passed, and the forensic team packed up and left the house.

In the driveway, Jake and Nick headed toward her.

"We found something you need to see." Nick held up three small plastic evidence bags. "They were found in Emma's dresser." He handed the bags to her.

Lexi took them and froze. "These are notes from Adam to Emma."

CHAPTER FOUR

*T*his can't be happening again. It was his handwriting.

The notes from Adam to Emma played on repeat in Lexi's mind.

Emma, we need to talk.
Adam

Can you meet me tonight?
Adam

Let's get together.
Adam

Why was her soon-to-be husband meeting with the woman? Fear coursed through her veins, and she handed the evidence back to Nick, her hand shaking.

"I knew he was no good," Nick said, his accusation hanging heavy in the air.

Unimpressed by his remark, she gave him a hard stare. "Innocent until proven guilty. Don't forget that."

"Then why does Emma have notes from Adam in her dresser?" Jake asked.

An angry knot formed in her stomach. She didn't appreciate feeling as if she was being interrogated by her partner.

"We can pull his phone records and see if they've been in contact," Nick said in a suggestive tone. "I think they were seeing each other."

Her heart sped up. Adam wasn't having an affair. He was wrong. There had to be a logical explanation.

"I bet he was sleeping with her, and she wanted to end things," Nick added, his words dripping with cynicism.

Lexi snapped. "How original, coming from you of all people. Are you serious?"

"It happens more than you think," Jake said, side-eyeing Nick.

Her tolerance ran out, and she got in her partner's face. "You're supposed to have my back. Not agree with his absurd theories."

Jake raised his hands in surrender. "We wouldn't be doing our job if we weren't exploring every possible angle."

Her blood boiled. "That doesn't include baseless accusations. I'm sure there's a reasonable explanation."

Nick's mouth tightened. "Like what?"

"You're both enjoying this, aren't you?" She clenched her teeth, sick of Nick's strong opinions. They glared at each other. "Maybe Adam was working on a story or had business with Carl Blunt. Have you thought of that? You already have him condemned without a shred of solid evidence."

"It's obvious he's guilty of something," Nick said,

his tone dismissive.

Lexi laughed at his absurd comment. "It's not obvious at all."

"You just don't want to see it." he continued. "The guy has never been right for you. Even Jake agrees with me."

"I'm not listening to this nonsense anymore. Screw this." Fuming, she walked away, raised her hand, and flipped them off, making her feelings clear. Nick mumbled something, but she couldn't make out what he said. She didn't care. They were wrong. Adam wasn't a cheater, and he wasn't a killer. Composing herself, she made her way back up to the house and knocked on the door again.

A minute later, the door opened, and Carl appeared, his eyes damp and bloodshot.

She felt like crying herself. "I'm sorry to bother you again. I need to ask you something that might help us figure out what happened to your daughter."

"You can, but I don't know anything," he said, his voice heavy with grief.

Her heart raced. "Did Emma ever mention a man by the name of Adam Quinn?"

His eyes narrowed. "Is he the one who killed her?"

Her voice was more forceful than she wanted it to be. "No. We're trying to piece together her last movements."

"What does it matter now?" Carl's face turned red with anger. "Emma is dead. Nothing is going to bring her back."

Lexi empathized with his pain. "You want justice for her, don't you?"

"Damn right, I do. This should never have happened."

"Then please, does the name Adam Quinn ring a bell?"

He remained silent for a long moment, thinking, then shook his head. "The name isn't familiar."

Lexi kept pressing, knowing it was a long shot. "Maybe you fixed his car? It's a black BMW I4 Grand Coupe."

Again, he shook his head. "I would have remembered a fancy car like that."

After they finished the conversation, Lexi walked back to her vehicle in deep thought. Thankfully, Nick and Jake had left. The last thing she wanted to do was talk to them. There was a more pressing conversation on her mind. She had to speak with Adam as soon as possible. The case just became personal. At the same time, she couldn't allow her personal feelings to cloud her professional judgment.

#

Back at the FBI office, Lexi settled behind her desk and found a hot cup of coffee and a warm apple fritter waiting for her, courtesy of Jake, a peace offering. The office was mostly silent with only the faint sounds of typing emanating from a few diligent agents working late.

She devoured the fritter, relishing the sweet treat. Logging into the National Crime Information

Center database, Lexi initiated a search for missing women in Michigan within the specified age range and impatiently drummed her fingers on the desk while waiting for the results. The computer beeped, and a list of one hundred and twenty-six potential matches scrolled down the screen. They were daughters, mothers, friends. She double-clicked on each name, scrutinizing the details and the missing women's faces. Most weren't college students, and many had been missing for over a decade.

Getting nowhere, she entered her credentials into ViCAP, the Violent Criminal Apprehension Program database used to analyze violent crimes and identifying patterns. Armed with the limited information she had on the victims and the killer, she set her search criteria, hoping to uncover any similarities or connections.

Jake approached her desk casually and leaned against the cubicle. "How's the fritter?"

She took a gulp of her coffee, savoring the much-needed caffeine boost. "Delicious. Thanks."

An awkward silence hung between them.

He jammed his hands into the pockets of his black tactical pants. "Hey, I'm sorry, Lexi. We have to consider every angle. That's all I was saying. I didn't mean to upset you."

She glanced at two agents at the next workstation staring at her, then back to Jake. "What's clear to me is your dislike for Adam and your belief in what Nick said. I expected your support. Nick is a jerk, and you know it. He'll do anything to tarnish Adam's reputation, hoping I'll change my mind about marrying him. That sure as hell isn't going to happen. You, of all people, know what he's like."

Jake frowned. "You have to admit the situation is suspicious."

Feeling like they were talking in circles, Lexi resisted the urge to bang her head against the wall. "I'm not jumping to any conclusions. Until we have all the facts, it's not worth discussing. We've got work to do. While I'm checking out a few things, how about you visit the Crave Haven Club and see what you can learn about Emma from her co-workers?"

Jake nodded. "By the way, Carl Blunt's alibi checked out."

"I'm not surprised," she said, glancing at him. "And for the record, a fritter and coffee won't fix things between us."

He touched her arm. "I really am sorry."

When he walked away, a sense of dread washed over her. She needed answers from Adam and couldn't wait to see him. Gazing at her desk and the towering stack of paperwork, Lexi realized the night was far from over. She delved into the first fifty entries on the list of possible similar crimes displayed on her screen and carefully examined each one. An hour and a half passed, and her cell phone rang.

It was Jake. In the background, dance music

blasted, its beat fast and energetic. "Did you find out anything?"

"The day before Emma disappeared, the bartender noticed a man acting suspiciously. He had been at the club a few times. Another co-worker witnessed her getting into the same man's car when she was out having a smoke."

Her pulse quickened. "Did you get a description?"

"About six-one, dark brown hair, and blue eyes. I wanted to check the security footage, but the club's system has been down for the past two weeks." He paused briefly. "Lexi, it's Adam. The bartender described the exact small cross tattoo on his right ring finger."

The air vanished from her lungs, and she couldn't breathe.

"There's more. He was driving a black BMW."

Lexi couldn't speak.

"Are you still there?"

Adam couldn't possibly be a killer. She had to keep it together. "Anything else?"

"Emma's car is still parked behind the club. The bartender said she left with the man on Wednesday morning, around twelve-thirty. That was the last time anyone saw her. I have to inform Nick about Adam. I don't have a choice."

It was all too much to process. She needed time. "Hold off until morning. I have to speak with Adam."

"What if you're in danger?"

His words made her flinch. What if Adam had

been leading a double life and she had been living with a killer? The thought stabbed her like an icy knife, sending shivers through her. "I'm asking you as my partner and friend, please, give me until morning."

Silence stretched over the line.

"You've got until morning then we bring him in for questioning."

Lexi heard enough. "I have to go." The world crumbled around her, and her phone slipped from her hand onto the desk. Adam couldn't be involved. It was impossible. She picked up the phone and sent him a text message.

> Lexi: I'm on my way home. See you soon.
> Adam: Dinner awaits...and wine :)

Swiftly saving the search results, Lexi logged out and gathered her belongings. She rushed out of the office, aware of what she had to do.

#

Twenty minutes later, Lexi stepped inside the house with her Glock 9mm securely holstered at her hip. Adam greeted her with a warm smile and a generous glass of her favorite Chardonnay. Despite the comfort of home, she couldn't shake the emotions swirling inside her. Shedding her coat, she felt increasingly apprehensive, unsure of how to broach the topic of Emma Blunt.

"It looks like your day took a turn for the worse," Adam said, sensing her nervousness, and handed her the glass of wine.

"Worse than you know."

"How about you tell me about it while we have dinner?" He kissed her forehead. "I'm happy you're home. I missed you."

"Me too." Lexi took a drink of her wine and followed him into the kitchen. Seated at the island, she watched him load her plate with all her favorite dishes: Kung Pao chicken, sweet and sour pork, egg rolls, and fried rice. Then he served himself.

A prolonged silence settled between them, and she picked at her food, her appetite long gone. "Can we talk?"

"Sure." He put his fork down. "What's up?"

She took a deep breath and exhaled slowly. "Are you having an affair?"

His jaw muscles flexed, taken aback by her accusation. "How can you ask me that?"

"Believe me, I didn't want to."

"I don't understand. Where's this coming from? Is Nick putting ridiculous thoughts in your head? I'm not your ex-husband and never will be. I love you too much to ever hurt you. For God sakes, we're getting married soon."

"Who is Emma Blunt?"

His jaw dropped. "She's a woman I've been interviewing for a story I'm doing for the paper next month."

Relief washed over her, and Lexi felt a brief flicker of hope. "Adam, she's one of the victims at the lake."

"That's awful." His brows furrowed, deepening the lines on his forehead. "How?"

Her gaze drifted to the cross tattoo on his finger

he got in college. "She was strangled. You were likely the last person to see her alive."

Fear flickered in the back of his eyes. "I know how this looks. You know me better than anyone. Do you believe I'm a serial killer?"

"It doesn't matter what I think."

"Dammit, Lexi. It matters to me."

She heard the tone change in his voice. The damage was done. "Tomorrow morning, you'll be brought in for questioning. I couldn't stop it. I tried."

"Do I need a lawyer?"

"It might be a good idea to consult one." His deflated expression tore at her heart.

"Whatever you think."

He sounded as scared as she felt. She drained her wine and poured another glass. "Tell me about the story you're working on."

"It's about the college call girl industry."

"What? Emma was a call girl?"

Adam swallowed, nodding. "She was trying to pay for nursing school and save for a condo. Her job as a server at the club wasn't enough."

"Did you interview any other women from the club?"

He nodded again. "Three others. Paris Wilson, Olivia Brown, and a girl who preferred I call her Rose."

She thought for a moment, processing everything. "How did you and Emma first meet?"

"A couple of weeks ago, I received an anonymous

phone tip that the Crave Haven Club was operating a call girl service behind the scenes, targeting college students. I hung out at the club a couple of times, and Emma agreed to speak with me, only on her terms. She was extremely cautious."

"Do you know if any of the other women attended Northwestern?"

"They all did. I met Emma for the first time on Monday night, then again on Tuesday. On Wednesday, I met with her and the others."

Lexi recalled him working late on those days, which wasn't unusual given his line of work, especially if a tip came in.

"The bartender said Emma got into your car around twelve-thirty on Wednesday morning."

"Sounds about right. We went to a coffee shop nearby and met the other girls. After the interviews, Emma said she would catch a ride with them back to her car at the club. I left and came home. That was the last time I spoke with any of them."

"I'll need a description of Rose." Lexi took a sip of her wine and set the glass down. "Your notes to Emma were found in one of her dresser drawers."

"It's kind of odd she would keep them. I used to leave them on her car windshield. It was how she wanted things done. Then she would text me with a date and time to meet." Worry etched his face. "This doesn't look good."

Lexi had never seen him so vulnerable and frightened. She needed to focus on the facts, refusing to let the man she loved be condemned for something he didn't do. "They'll be a record of the text messages. You haven't done anything wrong. Tell me everything you remember about your meetings with the women."

"I listened to their stories about what drove them to get into the business. Emma was a smart, ambitious girl who wanted a better life and needed money to do that. She talked about her father and her mother who passed away. The others weren't as forthcoming, but they were starting to trust me."

"Did they mention any dangerous clients or anyone who made them feel scared?"

"Not to me. The women were street-smart and knew exactly what they were getting into. Being call girls wasn't a big deal. To them, it was a temporary job, a cash injection."

Lexi blew out a worried breath. "We have to get ahead of this. I need to review your notes before Nick and Jake get their hands on them."

"They're on my laptop in the spare room." Adam squeezed the bridge of his nose. "What happens now?"

"Your car will likely be seized for processing." She glanced around their home, the three-bedroom ranch they bought together. She loved the floor-to-ceiling bookcases, the spacious open-concept kitchen, and the sprawling living room. It was the perfect home to raise a family, and they had planned on starting that family next year. "They'll search the house too."

"Whatever it takes to clear me." His voice faltered. "I'm sorry you've been dragged into this."

"We'll figure it out." She replayed the details of the murders in her mind. "Why do you think the women were killed?"

Adam fixed her with a long look. "They might have been targeted because they knew too much about the call girl operation."

"Someone is profiting from the girls. Did any of them give you the name of the person running the show?"

He shook his head. "They weren't willing to give up that information, especially Rose. She seemed jumpy. I swear I had nothing to do with this."

Lexi squeezed his hand. "I believe you, but I need to find out who did."

"I'll help however I can. It doesn't feel great being a suspect."

The only suspect. Her shoulders strained at the thought. The killer was still out there, and Lexi had a terrible feeling the worst was yet to come.

CHAPTER FIVE

E arly the next morning, fueled by three cups of coffee, Lexi dialed Jake's number and left a message, hoping he was able to uncover the true identity of Rose. After the call, she spoke with the medical examiner and provided him with the names of the two women Adam had interviewed in case they were the other victims. Then, she watched in horror as Adam's car was loaded onto a flatbed, and the crime scene team combed through their home. The images haunted her, and she couldn't shake them from her mind.

According to Adam's laptop notes, Paris Wilson was driven by a desperate desire to escape to California and immerse herself in the world of acting. Olivia Brown, a spirited rebel sought acceptance in the call girl industry, defying her strict upbringing. However, there was little information about Rose, other than she attended Northwestern. Something was off about this case. Her intuition was never wrong.

At the sheriff's department an hour later, Nick finished interrogating Adam and met her in the hallway. "What the hell was that back there?" Lexi asked, her tone sharp.

"They call it an interrogation for a reason."

"I've observed you questioning suspects before. That was a deliberate attack."

"We have to ask the tough questions. It's not personal."

"Cut the crap. You've had it out for Adam since day one."

"You're wrong. I'm trying to solve this case. By the way, you look like hell."

"How did you expect me to look? Are you satisfied now?"

"I'm still not buying his story."

Lexi grew angrier by the second. She wanted to slap him just for being annoying. "Seriously, Nick? How much evidence do you need? Adam willingly provided his DNA, and the techs unit won't find a damn thing in the house or his car because he's innocent."

"I'm still not completely convinced. Something doesn't smell right."

"Maybe that smell is the stench of your cheap cologne."

His eyes narrowed. "You don't need to insult me."

"Then stop insulting my intelligence. If I thought for one second that Adam was the killer, I'd bring him in myself."

Silence hung heavy between them, and he continued to stare at her. "If Adam isn't our guy, and Carl Blunt isn't, who is?"

Lexi wasn't in the mood to deal with him. She was tired, and her eyes burned from the lack of sleep. "I don't know but I will find him. Back the hell off and get on with your life. I'm marrying Adam. No more visits to my home, casual phone calls, or flowers. I'm watching you. If you step out of line again, I'll take you down." With that, she stormed down the hallway, leaving his mouth gaping open. Satisfied with her assertiveness, Lexi smiled to herself. The ball was now in his court. If he persisted with his predatory behavior or harassed Adam in any way, she would file a complaint with his superiors.

Her phone rang. She answered it and continued walking. "Agent Stone."

"Lexi, it's Michael Chen. Paris Wilson and Olivia Brown are your other victims. Their parents identified them about an hour ago."

"At least they now have names," she murmured to herself, feeling for the women's families.

"The bodies were in a state of mild to moderate decomposition, consistent with a time of death estimated at approximately thirty-six to forty-eight hours before discovery."

"What's the timeline?"

"I would say between late Wednesday night to early Friday morning."

The facts deepened her understanding of the monster they were dealing with. "Three kills in forty-eight hours. Our guy has been busy."

"Emma died first, followed by Olivia and Paris. Olivia and Paris were killed within a few hours of each other. My examination revealed multiple neck injuries, consistent with manual strangulation. No drugs or alcohol were detected in the preliminary toxicology tests. The sock and shoe found at the scene don't match any of the victims' foot sizes. Also, none of the victims were sexually assaulted."

Lexi was relieved the killer wasn't driven by sexual gratification. "Did Paris or Olivia have any religious tattoos like Emma?"

"No, but there is something else. Traces of fiberglass, likely from a boat or watercraft, were found in the tissue samples. The same traces were present on the crosses."

Her pulse quickened. "He probably owns a boat or has access to one. That's how he disposes of the bodies."

"It seems likely. I'll send you the reports."

She was about to end the call when another call came through. "Jake, what is it?"

"Another body turned up."

"What?" The news left her reeling. "Where?"

"Houghton Lake. I just sent you the details."

Her phone beeped, and she read the message. A female body washed up on Sullivan Beach, discovered by a woman walking her two dogs. The cause of death bore similarities to the previous victims. Lexi raced down the stairs and bolted out the back door of the building. "Meet me there."

Pocketing her phone, she scrambled into her SUV. Was the latest victim Rose or someone else? Lexi stomped on the gas pedal and sped out of the parking lot, realizing what they were up against. They had a fourth body and were no closer to finding the killer. They desperately needed a win.

#

Lexi arrived at Sullivan Beach ninety minutes later and spotted Jake with a group of local cops gathered near a brightly colored playground. Empty swings swayed in the wind. The beach was a drastic difference to the summer bustle enjoyed by anglers, boaters and campers. After flashing her ID at a stone-faced male officer guarding the cordoned-off section of the beach, she slipped under the police tape. Jake hurried over to her with his hands buried in his coat pockets. He looked stressed.

"Where's Nick?" she asked, looking around.

"He said he had something to do and would be late. Heard you gave him a piece of your mind," Jake said with a hint of amusement.

"He deserved it," Lexi retorted, pulling on a pair of latex gloves. Nick was no longer her concern. She had a job to do. "What do we have?"

Jake nodded toward a body about twenty yards away in the sand. "Female, mid-twenties. The M.E. won't be here for another forty minutes. Same MO as before. At least her eyes are intact."

Lexi approached the body, her boot heels sinking in the sand, deepening the sinking feeling in her gut. Stopping, she leaned over the corpse. Clouded, vacant eyes stared back at her. The dead woman resembled a discarded mannequin, her skin weathered and plastic-like from the elements. She bore lacerations and abrasions on her neck. Thick ropes secured her arms and legs to the wooden cross, and the same type of four orange flotation devices were attached to it, like the others.

"This is our guy," Lexi said, noting the similarities.

"The local cops have started canvassing the area."

Another life lost and another family left in ruins. For a brief moment, she felt defeated. "We have to get this guy off the streets. Any updates on Rose, the mystery woman?"

Jake shook his head. "With three victims tied to the Crave Haven Club, nobody's talking. The club's owner, Vincent Ramirez, has a long criminal record and connections to the underworld. The major crimes unit had their eye on him a few years back, but it never went anywhere. There's nothing directly linking him to these murders."

"Dig deeper. Follow the money. If Ramirez is our guy, there has to be a money trail."

"I'll get right on it," Jake said.

Lexi exhaled sharply and stared at the victim. She matched Adam's description of Rose. Pulling out her phone, she snapped a photo of the woman's face and sent it to him, accompanied by a brief message.

A minute later, her phone buzzed. "That's her," the message read, and she slid her phone back into her coat pocket. "It's Rose. Someone has to know who she is."

"I'll head back to the club and give it another shot."

In the distance, sirens grew louder, heralding the imminent arrival of the Evidence Response Team. It wouldn't be much longer before the tranquil beach would be transformed into an active crime scene.

"While you're doing that, I'll handle Williams. We don't need him breathing down our necks," Lexi said.

"Catch up with you a bit later."

After he left, Lexi sent a quick text message to Adam, updating him on the latest developments. Moments later, her gaze fixated on the lake as if it held the answers she desperately needed. All the women Adam had interviewed were dead. This didn't look good for him, and worry bubbled up inside her. Her thoughts were interrupted by Nick rushing toward her.

"We have to talk," he said in an urgent tone.

"What's going on?"

"It's about Adam."

"Not this again." She rolled her eyes and walked past him. He grabbed her arm, stopping her. "We've already had this conversation. We aren't doing it again."

"You need to listen. He's going to be arrested."

Her legs froze. "For what?"

Nick's gaze locked onto hers. "The murder of Olivia Brown."

"You're insane." She shook free of his grasp. "Adam would never—"

"His DNA, along with a piece of rope, was found in Olivia Brown's apartment. The lab confirmed it matches the rope used to bind the victims to the crosses. He was there, Lexi. More evidence is bound to surface, linking him to the murders. It's only a matter of time."

Denial surged through her, threatening to tear her apart. For a split second, she felt lightheaded. "That's impossible. He never visited her apartment. He wasn't in any of the victims' homes. They met at the Mug and Mingle coffee shop. It doesn't make sense. It has to be a mistake."

"The facts don't lie. Neither does DNA," Nick said, cutting her off. "I know it's hard to believe. The evidence is what it is."

The world closed in around her. The man she loved, a serial killer? She had trusted Adam completely, given him her heart. Did she truly know him? Lexi bent over and threw up in the sand. After she was done, she straightened and replayed their relationship in her mind from the first time they met. "It can't be true."

Nick looked her in the eye. "I'm sorry."

"I doubt that," she said angrily and brushed past him, rushing back to the SUV.

How could she move forward with their wedding, their life together? She had believed Adam was innocent of any wrongdoing. Nothing in his body language had told her anything different. Her mind raced, questioning everything she thought she knew. Had she been wrong all along? Uncertainty gripped her, and Lexi realized her life was about to change.

#

At the sheriff's department, Lexi peered through the two-way glass at Adam, his hands cuffed in front of him. Her stomach churned with a mixture of dread and disbelief. Could Adam truly be involved with the murders? Was she wrong about him? Had she missed something? The thought left her shaken.

"Your DNA was found in Olivia Brown's apartment on a glass in her living room. You were there," Nick said.

"That's not true. I've told you everything."

Nick continued in his accusatory tone. "We found a piece of rope too, the same rope used to bind the victims to those wooden crosses you made."

Her gaze lingered on Adam, searching for any sign of guilt or deceit. His face revealed nothing.

"What crosses? I had nothing to do with the murders. You've got the wrong guy," Adam insisted, his voice edged with frustration.

Nick's aggression escalated. He slammed his fist onto the table. Lexi flinched at the sudden outburst, and she felt Adam's fear radiate through the glass.

"I'm telling you the truth."

Nick leaned in closer, his expression menacing. "You're lying."

"I'm telling the goddamn truth."

Her heart ached for Adam, torn between wanting to defend him and the nagging doubts creeping into her mind. She had to let the interrogation play out, despite her inner turmoil.

"We know you were involved. You strangled Olivia Brown and dumped her body in the lake and then you did the same to the other victims. You're one sick prick."

Adam's demeanor never changed. There was no

hint of guilt, only fear and frustration. Doubts stabbed at Lexi's core.

"Give me a polygraph test, and take one yourself," Adam said, his voice cutting through the tension. "You framed me."

His accusation stunned her. Could Nick be capable of framing Adam? Could he be the real killer?

Nick's fury flared. "Don't turn this on me, buddy. It's your DNA, not mine."

"Who better to frame me than the ex-husband who's been stalking his ex-wife for years? You could have plucked a glass from anywhere I've been and planted it. You have my DNA on file, remember? I'd say things aren't looking too good for you."

Lexi's head spun with uncertainty, torn between her loyalty to Adam and the evidence. At this point, could she even trust her own instincts? Was Adam a master manipulator, trying to deceive her too?

Adam looked in her direction again. "Lexi, I know you can hear me. I didn't kill anyone."

"You're looking at a death sentence," Nick reminded him.

Adam glared at him, his eyes narrow slits. "I want a lawyer. Better get yourself one too."

Lexi stepped back from the two-way glass. She couldn't trust the evidence, couldn't trust Nick or Adam.

Nick burst out of the interrogation room, his nostrils flaring. "He's lying."

"I'm not so sure. There's something off about the whole situation."

"You're letting your emotions cloud your judgment. Exactly why you shouldn't be on the case. The evidence speaks for itself."

It was her duty to investigate the case thoroughly. If she didn't, she wouldn't be doing her job. "What if there's more to this? What if the evidence was planted by the real killer? We haven't even had a chance to investigate the owner of the club. We owe it to the victims' families to be certain we've got the right person."

"Face it, Lexi. We've got our guy." Nick stormed out of the interrogation room, leaving her alone with her thoughts.

Accepting Adam as the killer meant a future without him. Lexi headed down the hall to the evidence locker. She filled out the necessary paperwork and logged out Emma Blunt's laptop, determined to uncover the truth, regardless of where it led her.

CHAPTER SIX

Thirty minutes later, Lexi parked outside the FBI office, replaying Adam's interrogation in her mind, her stomach a hard knot. The evidence against him didn't make sense. Nick's anger about her impending marriage made him a likely suspect. She climbed out of the vehicle with Emma's laptop tucked under her arm and hurried into the building.

Rushing to her desk, she ignored her colleagues' questioning glances. It was clear everyone knew about Adam by their stares scrutinizing her. The implications of his arrest would attract unwanted media attention, and her professional reputation would be at stake. After taking off her coat, she plugged in Emma's laptop and let it boot up. There was no doubt in her mind she had to speak with Williams before he hunted her down.

As she walked down the hallway to his office, her pulse raced. Lexi stuck her head inside the door. He was seated behind his desk. One wall of the office had awards and photographs of high-ranking officials who had played a significant role in shaping the Bureau. The FBI seal was painted on the other wall, values every agent held dear: "Fidelity, Bravery,

Integrity."

"Just the person I wanted to see. Take a seat, Agent Stone," he said, motioning to one of the chairs in front of his desk.

Lexi sat down, her nerves on edge, and focused on the carpet's brown geometric pattern. "I'm sure you've heard about Adam Quinn. He's being arraigned tomorrow."

"Brody has already filled me in."

She swallowed hard. "I believe Adam's been framed. The evidence isn't adding up."

Leaning forward, his expression turned serious. "Do you have any solid proof he was framed?"

"Not yet, but I will. Please keep this between us for now."

He arched an eyebrow, confused. "Why exclude your partner and Brody?"

"I can't say at the moment. Sir, please trust me. I've never failed this office, and I'm not about to start now."

He studied her intensely for a few seconds. "" have concerns about your impartiality, as does Detective Brody. He wants you off the case due to your personal involvement with Quinn."

She held back her annoyance. "With all due respect, I disagree. My duty is to the truth. I took an oath, and I stand by it. All I'm asking for is the chance to uncover what's really going on."

A few minutes of tense silence enveloped the room.

"If you compromise this case in any way, you're

off it."

Lexi nodded, satisfied. "Thank you. I won't let you down." She left his office, more determined than ever to clear Adam's name.

Back at her desk, a hand touched her shoulder, and she jumped.

"Hey, are you okay?" Jake asked. "I just heard about Adam. It's unbelievable. I'm here for you if you want to talk."

Her mouth dried up, and she fought to control her emotions. "I don't want to discuss it."

Could she even trust her partner, considering his feelings about Adam? Lexi wasn't convinced. She suddenly felt alone.

Jake settled at his desk. "Is Williams keeping you on the case?"

"Nick wanted me off, but I guess Williams trusts my judgment." Lexi started searching Emma's social media posts and looked up to see Jake staring at her. "What?"

"Our victim from Sullivan Beach. Her name is Samantha Reed."

"Can you contact the M.E. and let him know?"

He pulled out his cell phone from his pocket ready to make the call. "What are you working on?"

"A long shot. I'm hoping Emma's files hold something crucial to the case."

"Are you sure you don't want to talk about Adam?"

Lexi met his gaze head-on. She couldn't. Not now. "I'm positive."

"What's going on? This isn't like you." His brows furrowed. "The guy you're about to marry has been arrested for murder."

"What do you want me to do? Fall apart in front of everyone? Would that make you feel better? I'm doing my job, trying to track down a killer. How about you investigate the club's finances?"

"I didn't mean it like that," he said, raising his hands. "I'm just saying I'm worried about you."

Lexi sighed. "I know, and I'm sorry. Everything is happening so fast. I don't know what to believe anymore."

"I get it. If you want to talk later, we can grab a drink."

She managed a small smile. "Thanks."

While he called the M.E.'s office, she continued combing through the folders on Emma's hard drive, desperate to find any evidence to clear Adam.

As the day progressed, aggravation consumed her. She found nothing substantial, just social media connections between the women, including Samantha Reed. Re-examining the case file, the kayaker's statements, and the forensics turned up nothing. They were no closer to finding out what happened to the women or who was responsible.

"Hungry?" Jake asked, breaking the silence.

Lexi's stomach growled. She couldn't remember the last time she had eaten anything substantial. "I could go for a burger from the place down the street."

"I'll go."

She nodded absentmindedly, her thoughts on Adam. It was ten o'clock, and normally he'd be at home waiting for her, but this wasn't a typical day. Far from it. Instead, he was locked up in a cold cell at the sheriff's department. There was nothing she could do except hope that the judge gave him bail so she could talk with him without putting her job in jeopardy. Rubbing the back of her neck, she turned her attention to the ViCap search results she'd saved from the day before. Bringing up the file on the screen, she began reading through the cases, laser-focused on the details. Twenty minutes later, Jake returned with their food.

"I got you an extra-large coffee. Figured you could use it." He set the coffee and food on her desk.

Lexi glanced up. "Thanks."

Sitting at his workstation, Jake unwrapped his burger and took a hearty bite.

Eating her burger and munching on some French fries, she continued reading, determined to find out if Emma Blunt was the killer's first victim.

Hours blurred by.

Frustrated and ready to call it a day, one particular case caught her eye. A woman by the name of Victoria Ryder had been found tied to a wooden cross floating in Alum Creek Lake in the same area where Jake and Adam had grown up in Columbus, Ohio. Her pulse quickened. She scrolled, searching for the name of the detective in charge of the case.

Matthew Ryder? Lexi felt the blood drain from her

face.

Her eyes darted to her partner, working quietly across from her. Why hadn't he mentioned the case, or that his father was the lead investigator? What else was he keeping from her?

Jake's voice sliced through her thoughts. "Is something wrong?"

The evidence pointed to Adam as Olivia Brown's killer. Nick had a motive to frame him, and her partner was hiding things from her. Everything was wrong. Her stomach churned, and she thought she was going to be sick. Remaining calm, she lied, "Just wondering about the club's finances."

"I'm no expert. On paper, Crave Haven appears legit. Everything seems to be on the up and up." He reclined in his chair and stretched his arms above his head. "I'll get Steve Michaels from Financial Crimes working on it. None of the women I spoke to at the club are willing to come forward about the call girl service. They're scared."

"They should be. Four women are dead, and there could be more," Lexi said, realizing she was alone in proving Adam's innocence. "I think I'm going to head home and start fresh in the morning."

"I've got some paperwork to finish up. Get some rest. If you need anything, call me."

Lexi grabbed her laptop and coat and headed to the elevator, her mind swirled with emotions. As soon as Adam was arraigned, she would visit the club to make sure Jake hadn't tampered with any evidence. It didn't sit well, having three men in her life, none of whom she felt she could trust.

#

The next morning, Lexi stood in front of the courthouse downtown. Cool morning air nipped at her cheeks. Despite the early hour, the scene was packed with dozens of reporters from news outlets all over the country, each jostling for a position with their cameras and microphones. The constant barrage of questions made her head spin. The press thrived on sensationalism and scandal. Lexi knew they would stop at nothing to get their story. She had experienced their intimidation in the past during the failed kidnapping case. This was something else entirely.

A pushy newswoman, her brown eyes blazing with excitement, thrust a microphone in her face. "Agent Stone. When did you realize your fiancé was a killer?"

Her hands clenched at the insinuation. Lexi had to keep her composure if she was going to get through this. Brushing past the woman, she ignored the question and pushed her way through the tall glass doors and into the courthouse.

Inside the courtroom, symbols of justice were everywhere, from the scales carved into the dark wood paneling to the gavel on the judge's bench. The atmosphere was no less tense. Wooden benches creaked with the weight of curious onlookers and journalists. Lexi found a seat, and her eyes locked on Nick, seated in the row across from her. He had a sour look on his face. Her hands curled into fists in her lap. Where was Jake? Why wasn't he here?

A stern-looking man with a thick red beard and a deep voice strode in. "Good morning. You may be seated," the judge said in an authoritative voice.

When the room settled, a door swung open, and a sturdy-looking deputy, as wide as he was tall, led Adam in with his hands cuffed in front of him. Lexi's heart ached at the dark shadows under his eyes and his defeated appearance. She couldn't offer reassurance now, even if she wanted to. His eyes brightened briefly upon seeing her. The man she loved faced a crime that could send him to death row or imprison him for life. The clock was ticking. She had to find the real killer.

After the deputy undid the handcuffs, Adam sat next to his lawyer and shot him a panicked look. Dressed in an expensive tailored brown suit, William Hutz was a legend, renowned for getting his clients off in the most challenging of cases. He tossed his leather briefcase on the table and shot her a nod. At eight-hundred dollars an hour, he'd better be worth every penny.

The prosecutor rose, his bald head gleaming under the natural light filtering through the windows. His intense gaze was fixed on the judge. "Your honor, The State of Michigan brings charges against Adam Quinn for the brutal murder of Olivia Brown. The evidence is clear: the defendant's DNA was found in Miss Brown's apartment, and he was the last person to see her alive."

The court reporter's fingers tapped against the stenotype machine, capturing every word. Lexi remained calm, knowing the prosecutor was grasping at straws, trying to make the evidence fit his narrative. She had already contacted the FBI's Digital Analysis and Research Center before leaving the house and discovered Adam's car's GPS data didn't place him anywhere near the victims' homes or in the vicinity of the lakes at the time of the murders. He was innocent.

The judge's voice echoed again through the room. "How does your client plead?"

Adam stood, his eyes darting frantically as if searching for an escape. "Not guilty."

Lexi bit her lip and shifted on the bench. She couldn't take the uncertainty. The judge had to get it right.

"The preliminary hearing will be scheduled for two weeks from now. In the meantime, make sure your cases are prepared thoroughly. No grandstanding, Mr. Hutz. Mr. Quinn, you are charged with aggravated murder. The evidence presented against you is very serious," the judge continued. "However, you are entitled to a fair trial. Your standing in the community is impeccable. I don't believe you are a flight risk. Bail is set at two million dollars."

Gasps and murmurs filled the room. Nick shook his head at the judge's decision and stared at her.

They needed $200,000 to secure his release and would have to use their home as collateral.

Everything they had worked so hard for. Lexi's heart sank.

"You must surrender your passport and any firearms, report regularly, and remain in the state until your trial date," the judge added.

William Hutz nodded his agreement and patted Adam on the back. Afterward, Adam glanced over his shoulder at her, his eyes bursting with hope and uncertainty.

It was a small victory. Lexi gave him a reassuring smile. At least he could come home—for now.

Nick caught up with her in the hallway.

She opened her mouth to say something, but he cut her off.

"Quinn got lucky. I'm surprised the judge allowed bail."

He was irritated, and she knew it. "Luck has nothing to do with it."

"You really believe he's innocent, don't you? He's lying to you, Lexi."

"Williams gave me forty-eight hours to prove Adam was framed. I plan on doing just that."

Three hours later, Lexi left the courthouse with Adam, and they were immediately surrounded by reporters and photographers.

As they made their way to the parking lot, a reporter ran up beside them and pushed a microphone in Adam's face. "Are you the Lakeside Killer?"

Adam ignored her and kept walking with his head down.

"Mr. Quinn, care to comment on the murder charge against you?"

Lexi stepped in front of her and blocked her. "No comment."

The woman persisted and shot her a look. "Did you use your connections, Agent Stone, to get your fiancé out on bail?"

Irritation gave way to anger. "That's a ridiculous accusation. How dare you."

"Come on, the public deserves to know. It's news."

Lexi flung open the door and got in. Adam climbed in beside her and swore under his breath, registering his own annoyance. Drumming her fingers on the steering wheel, she kept her eyes on the rearview mirror and watched the reporter scuttle back to the courthouse like a rat. The media would stop at nothing to ruin Adam's life. She wouldn't let that happen. Lexi glanced at Adam staring out the window with his jaw clenched. He was as furious as she was, but he was always better at hiding his emotions.

"Hutz said I could go to prison for life, or worse."

"That's not going to happen."

"How can you be so sure?"

"Because you aren't alone in this. I have the one thing the prosecutor doesn't have."

"What's that?"

"Evidence and other suspects." Lexi started the engine and strapped her seatbelt across her chest. "You need to tell me everything you know about Jake and Victoria Ryder."

#

The ten-minute drive from the courthouse to the Crave Haven Club was torturous. Adam's silence only made things worse. Lexi was desperate for answers.

"Who is Victoria Ryder?" she finally asked.

He glanced at her briefly, then looked away. "It's been years since I've heard that name."

"Adam, you need to tell me."

He exhaled a shaky breath and looked down at his hands. "She was Jake's sister."

"Wait, what? He's never mentioned a sister."

"I started dating Victoria when we were sixteen and ended things with her during our first semester of college. She didn't take it well, spiraled out of control."

"What happened?"

He kept his eyes glued to the buildings passing by. "She became a call girl."

"Are you serious? And you decided to keep this from me? She wasn't just murdered. She was strangled and tied to a wooden cross like the recent victims."

He paused for a long moment and hung his head. "I'm sorry. I couldn't talk about her. She's the reason I became a journalist."

Lexi noted his discomfort, the strained emotion in his voice, and how he avoided her gaze. It was obvious he had been carrying around the guilt for years. How could he have kept something so important from her, especially when it was relevant to the case she was working on? Despite reminding herself he was human and wasn't perfect, the feeling of betrayal hurt, casting yet another doubt over her already turbulent relationship with the men in her life.

She noticed her white knuckles on the steering wheel, and her anger intensified. "Four call girls are dead, and you didn't think it was important to mention?"

"I'm sorry. I blamed myself for her death. If I hadn't ended things, maybe she would still be alive."

"What happened to her wasn't your fault. You didn't kill her. But Jake blamed you for her death. That's why you two aren't friends."

"We were best friends up until Victoria died. I'm sorry I didn't tell you sooner."

She took a deep breath and forced herself to calm down. "Did you inform your lawyer?"

He shook his head.

"You don't have a choice. Lives are at stake, including yours. You have to tell him. Why was Matthew Ryder leading the case?"

"Things were different back then. He was the first to arrive at the lake where Victoria's body was found."

She pulled up to a stop sign and glanced at him. "Discovering his daughter like that must have been horrific."

"It hit him hard. Three days later, Eric Pittman was arrested for her murder. The guy's a deeply disturbed religious fanatic who believes he's some kind of instrument of divine judgment. Victoria represented everything he considered immoral. He believed by subjecting her to a symbolic punishment, he would purify her. Pittman crafted the wooden cross at his family's farm, replicating the suffering of Jesus Christ. The guy's a real sicko."

"I need to find out if he was released from prison."

"I think he was."

"So, there's a chance he could have killed again," Lexi said, pondering out loud and watched a yellow and white cab zoom by.

"I guess it's a possibility."

The Crave Haven Club's building exuded exclusivity with its sleek modern lines and tinted glass windows. A metallic black and white sign with the letters C, H, and C towered above the entrance. Lexi shut off the engine, her stomach churning.

"What are we doing here?" Adam asked.

"I need to follow up on a few things. Nick and Jake both had motives to frame you. I can't ignore the possibility."

"You think Jake could be the killer? No way. He's your partner. My money's on Nick. The bastard would do anything to get rid of me."

His frustration matched hers. She couldn't ignore the nagging feeling in her gut. "Why would Jake cover up the Ohio case? He had a duty to speak up."

"Maybe he couldn't talk about it. Victoria's death

hit him hard. He lost his only sibling." He paused for a second. "Let's say you're right. What are you going to do about it?"

She took a minute and replayed her interactions with Nick and Jake in her mind, searching for anything that might shed light on the truth. Nick's animosity toward Adam was driven by a desire to eliminate him from the equation so he could step in. His desperation to see Adam behind bars made him a viable suspect, a dangerous one. She thought about the years of trust she had shared with her partner, and the countless cases they had solved together, which made her theory sound even crazier.

"They both fit the profile, and either of them could have rented a boat to dump the bodies. I need to get my hands on their vehicle's GPS data without their knowledge."

"Be careful, Lexi. If you're wrong, it could destroy your career."

She unbuckled her seatbelt, fully aware of what her decision could cost her. "I'm not going to watch you be wrongly accused while the real killer walks free."

CHAPTER SEVEN

Inside the Crave Haven Club, daylight cast a stark contrast against the metallic furnishings, polished to a gleaming shine. Neon lights raced along the ceiling throughout the deserted establishment. It was early afternoon, and a bartender in his late twenties, with a sculpted physique and colorful snake tattoos on both forearms, was wiping down the sleek metal counter. Above him, a towering DJ booth pulsed with a kaleidoscope of blinking lights.

Lexi's footsteps stomped across the expansive concrete dance floor, each stride fueling her mounting anger. The thought of Adam facing the consequences for crimes he didn't commit made her furious.

The bartender glanced up and greeted her with a charismatic smile. "What can I get for you?"

"Just water," Lexi said, her gaze briefly drawn to the man's good looks. "It's pretty quiet in here."

He removed the cap from an overpriced, square-bottled water she couldn't pronounce and set it in front of her. "It's always slow until around seven when things start picking up."

She showed him her credentials and noticed how

his intense green eyes darted toward the entrance before returning to meet her gaze. "I'd like to ask you a few questions."

"What's this about?"

She took a sip of water and set the bottle down, eyeing the glasses in a row on a shelf behind him. They looked identical to the glass found in Olivia Brown's apartment. She took a moment to form her thoughts. "I'm investigating the disappearance of one of the club's employees."

"You mean Emma?"

"How do you know she disappeared?"

"The waitresses haven't stopped talking about it. They're scared to death."

Lexi understood their fear. She had seen it before. The call girls were no exception. "Credible information suggests the perpetrator may have been a patron here."

He shrugged nonchalantly. "Can't help you there. People come and go all the time."

"Have you noticed anyone acting suspiciously recently? Maybe getting too cozy with Emma or the other female servers?"

He shook his head.

Confusion clouded her mind. According to Jake, the bartender had identified Adam as the suspicious man at the bar. "What about a guy with a cross tattoo on his finger?"

"No clue. Like I said, people come and go."

Lexi's chest squeezed. The man was either lying, or Jake had lied to her. There was only one way to find out. "I will be right back. I forgot my cell phone in my car."

A few minutes later, Lexi returned with Adam.

The bartender's eyes flashed with recognition. "I think you both should leave."

Adam intervened, his eyes hard. "You know who I am."

The man hesitated, staring at the tattoo on Adam's finger.

"We're not going anywhere. I have more questions," Lexi said. With each word, her voice grew louder. "You want to be on the right side of this, don't you?"

The man nodded.

"Good. Now what's your name?"

"Ryan Anderson."

She leaned in, her voice now modulating low and forceful. "I could arrest you right now unless you cooperate. We know about the call girls. Do the cameras work?"

His Adam's apple bobbed, and he swallowed hard, his eyes darting to one of the cameras in the corner of the room. He nodded again.

"The cameras weren't down for two weeks, were they?" Lexi's voice grew colder. "Obstructing a federal investigation has severe consequences. I need the truth."

Tension filled the air.

"Okay, they work. He told me to say they didn't."

Adam's voice came out as a low growl. "Who did?"

"Some FBI guy."

Adam exchanged glances with her, fury evident in his eyes. Her suspicions grew stronger. It had to be Jake. She had trusted him, relied on him. Pieces of the puzzle were beginning to fit. His involvement explained some of the missing answers. She wanted to confront him, to understand how he could have betrayed her, but she knew it was the wrong move.

She turned her attention back to Ryan. "I need to review the club's security footage. While you're at it, get me a list of all employees and regulars at the club."

The bartender nodded frantically, beads of sweat forming along his hairline. "I'll do whatever you want."

He went and locked the front door then led her and Adam to a large office tucked away in a corner of the club. The room was brightly lit with rows of monitors displaying camera feeds capturing the club's every corner, inside and out. The hum of electronic equipment filled the air.

"Start by showing me the security footage from the past week," Lexi said.

He navigated through the system, bringing up the requested footage.

Her gaze darted from one monitor to another. Five minutes passed, and she pointed to one of the screens. "There. Zoom in."

Ryan manipulated the controls until the image became crystal clear.

It can't be. Adam was at the bar, finished his drink, then left. Minutes later, Ryan grabbed the glass Adam had used and put it in an evidence bag. Ten minutes later, Jake arrived, and Ryan handed him the evidence. The ground beneath her seemed to shift, and her heart plummeted. "Is that the man who asked you to lie?"

"That's him." He glanced at Adam. "He told me to put the glass you were using into the bag, and he'd pick it up."

Adam's jaw clenched, his anger mingling with hers. "Jake set me up."

Lexi's chest heaved with each breath. She would have to contact the Office of Professional Responsibility, responsible for ensuring the conduct of FBI employees. It was a path she never thought she would have to take with her partner. "Can you make me a copy of the footage?"

"I think so." Several minutes later, Ryan found a thumb drive, made a copy, and handed it to her. "Am I in trouble?" His breath came out in short gasps, his eyes darting rapidly side to side.

Lexi pocketed the drive, barely able to keep her rage from surfacing. "That depends. Are you willing to give us a written statement about everything you know about Vincent Ramirez, the call girl service, and the FBI agent?"

He started to hyperventilate. "Ramirez will kill me if I say anything."

"The FBI can offer you protection," Lexi said. "But you have to help us first. We can put you in protective custody right now, and you'll start a new life elsewhere."

"Like witness protection or something?"

She nodded. "It's the only way out of this alive."

"What about my mother and sister? I can't leave without them. He'll come after them."

He was right. There was no doubt in her mind Ramirez would kill Ryan and his family. "We can put them in protective custody as well."

Silence enveloped the room for what seemed like forever before he finally said, "Okay, I'll give you everything you need."

She had to act swiftly to protect him. Reaching into her pocket, she retrieved her cell phone and made the call.

"Special Agent David Williams."

"Sir, it's Lexi." She paced back and forth, briefing him on the situation, omitting any mention of her partner's involvement.

"Take him to the safe house on Webster Street. I'll have a couple of agents grab his family. I'll have a team meet you there."

Her phone beeped, notifying her of the incoming text. She checked the message for the safe house's address and instructions. "There's something else. Jake and Nick can't know about this. I'll explain everything once I get Ryan out of harm's way. Adam Quinn was definitely set up. I have the physical evidence to prove it."

"Are you sure about this?"

"Positive, sir."

"Then your witness's safety and securing the evidence are top priority. Remain vigilant. I'm not losing any agents on my watch."

#

Twenty minutes later, Lexi steered into the driveway of the safe house nestled in the quiet working-class neighborhood. The home's beige-sided exterior and detached single garage blended seamlessly with the other houses on the street. Nervousness surged through her, and she scanned her surroundings twice before stepping out of the vehicle. Two male agents, dressed street-casual, greeted her and Ryan with a silent nod.

After Ryan was escorted safely inside, Lexi slid back behind the wheel, and Adam's face stiffened. "What are we going to do about Jake?"

Regrets flooded her mind, and she berated herself for her initial suspicion of Nick when the real threat was her partner. If only she had seen it sooner, she could have prevented Adam's arrest. She had entrusted Jake with her life, only to have everything unravel before her eyes.

Gritting her teeth, Lexi reversed out of the driveway. "I need to retrieve the GPS data from his SUV."

"How? You can't simply ask him for it."

Traffic surged forward, and she cursed herself for missing the subtle signs of Jake's true nature. The betrayal stung. "I have an FBI contact who owes me a favor. Jake won't suspect a thing."

Steering into the driveway of their home a few minutes later, Lexi shut off the engine and called her contact, a tech specialist proficient in cybersecurity and digital forensics who worked in the Digital Analysis and Research Center. He had the expertise to bypass and extract crucial information. After a couple of rings, he answered.

"Agent Miller."

Their long-standing friendship from their time at the FBI Academy kicked into gear. "Ace, it's Lexi. I need your help." She filled him in on the situation.

A brief pause preceded his response. "Your partner did all that? Jesus. Sounds like a real psycho."

"I need to extract the GPS data from his SUV without alerting him. Can you do it?"

"They don't call me Ace for no reason. I can manipulate the ignition system remotely, causing the engine to fail without raising any suspicion. Give me the location of his vehicle."

Lexi provided Jake's home address.

"What are you looking for from the data after his vehicle's towed to the garage?"

"I need to know if he was at any of the locations I just sent you." The idea her partner could be responsible for four murders was hard to accept. Lexi tried to dismiss the thought as absurd, but the evidence spoke volumes.

"I'll be in touch," Ace said. "Watch your back."

"Thanks. I owe you." She ended the call.

"Now what?" Adam asked.

Lexi unfastened her seatbelt. "We wait. Jake will probably contact me in the morning, looking for a ride to the office."

"You shouldn't handle this on your own. You need

to inform your boss, or I hate to say it, Nick. Jake's unpredictable and dangerous. He's already proved that."

She hesitated, weighing the risks of involving her SAC and Nick without concrete evidence linking Jake to the murders. It felt premature. "I need the GPS data before I make a move."

Adam stepped out of the SUV. Concern etched his face. "Promise me you won't confront Jake alone. Your safety comes first."

Lexi nodded. Jake had taken advantage of her and his position at the FBI. If another woman turned up dead, she would never forgive herself for failing to see the truth.

#

The next morning, a dreary charcoal-gray sky and heavy rain greeted Lexi after a restless night's sleep. She wasn't sure when she had finally fallen asleep. The man she had trusted with her life was now a potential cold-blooded killer. Dread weighed on her, imagining the moment she'd have to face her superiors, explaining how she had unknowingly worked alongside a killer. Anger surged through her veins, Jake's betrayal cutting deeper than any physical wound she'd experienced. To add to her misery, reporters were camped outside of the house. She was having a hard time concentrating on anything.

While Adam showered, she sat at the kitchen island, cradling a cup of coffee with both hands, and delved into the Victoria Ryder case. Crime scene photographs and reports flooded the laptop screen, unveiling the grisly details of the murder. Eric Pittman's menacing mugshot leered at her. Victoria's involvement in the sex industry had made her the target of Pittman's distorted sense of justice. Her heartbeat accelerated, and Lexi continued reading. Pittman had been released from prison nine years ago and was currently residing on his family's farm.

The shrill sound of her cell phone cracked the silence. Ace's name lit the screen, and her heart skipped a beat. "Hey, did you find anything?"

"His SUV wasn't anywhere near any of the crime scenes or the victims' homes during the medical examiner's timeframe. The data doesn't match. I'm sending you the file now."

"Jake isn't stupid. Either he picked up the women elsewhere or used a different vehicle. I'm leaning toward the latter." She pressed a few buttons and accessed the file on her phone, scrutinizing the geofencing data, travel history, timestamps, and locations.

"I did find something interesting," Ace said. "He visited a warehouse on West Front Street before and after each murder. Spent hours there each time."

The word "warehouse" hung in the air, and Lexi began connecting the dots. "It's his base of operation where he keeps a boat or another vehicle."

"Definitely worth investigating." Ace sent her the address.

"I'll reach out to Nick for backup," Lexi said,

thinking out loud.

"You mean Nick, your ex?"

"Yeah, don't even get me started on that one."

Ace chuckled, momentarily easing the tension. "I never liked the guy."

"You're not alone in that sentiment."

"Be careful, Lexi. If Jake suspects you're onto him, he won't hesitate to kill you. Four lives are already lost. One more means nothing to him."

His words sent a shiver through her. Deep down, she feared what Jake might do if he discovered she suspected him. "I'll watch my back. Thanks again."

"Keep me in the loop."

Ending the call, she placed her phone on the countertop.

Adam strolled into the kitchen dressed in jeans and a plain black T-shirt. His hair was wet and glistening. He poured a coffee.

Looking up from her cup, she met his gaze. "Ace tracked Jake's vehicle's movements before and after the murders. I think he used a different vehicle. It makes sense. He spent significant time at a warehouse."

His eyes narrowed with intensity. "We have to act fast."

Lexi took a sip of her coffee, and her cell phone rang again. She glanced at the screen, then at Adam, her heart pounding. "It's him."

"You've got this."

She steadied her trembling hand and answered the call.

"Hey. Can you pick me up?" Jake asked. "The damn SUV won't start. I've got a meeting with Steve Michaels at eight to go over the club's finances."

Her gaze darted to the clock on the microwave. Seven-fifteen. Taking a deep breath, she maintained her carefully composed tone. "Give me twenty minutes."

"Is everything okay? You sound different."

A knot formed in her throat, and she exchanged a glance with Adam. She couldn't afford to let her guard down or underestimate Jake for a second. "With everything going on with Adam and the horde of reporters outside the house, I'm just stressed."

There was a long pause on the other end.

"Have another coffee and I'll see you soon."

Setting the phone down, Lexi grimaced at the rain battering the kitchen windows. She rested her hand on Adam's arm. "I know you're angry. I see it in your eyes. What Jake did to you is unforgivable."

He exploded. "He framed me for murder, all to get back at me for Victoria's death. It's not just about what he did to me. You trusted him too. It was all a lie."

Her pulse pounded in her ears, and she berated herself for the hundredth time. Had the upcoming wedding pushed Jake over the edge? Why was he willing to risk everything including his career for revenge?

Her fists clenched. "He'll pay for what he's done." She knew there wasn't enough evidence to arrest him specifically for the murders. "Security footage only places him at the club, and Ryan Knight's testimony confirms he framed you. I need to find concrete evidence directly tying Jake to the murders."

"I'm going with you to the warehouse," Adam said.

She wasn't going to put him in the crossfire. Not a chance. "No, you're not. I want you to stay put. I'll contact Nick for backup."

"Lexi, I can't just sit here while you put yourself in danger."

She locked eyes with him, understanding his concern. "I'll be okay. You can help by writing the story. The truth needs to come out for Emma, the other women, and their families."

Silence fell over the room, and she witnessed the conflict in his eyes. He was torn between protecting her and ensuring Jake paid for his crimes.

Taking a deep breath, he finally said, "All right. Promise you'll be careful."

She closed the laptop lid and stood. "I promise." Reaching for her holster, she unfastened the strap and ejected the magazine, verifying it was fully loaded, then pulled back the slide, confirming a round was chambered. Lexi prayed she wouldn't have to use it.

CHAPTER EIGHT

J ake's heart thundered in his chest. Lexi would arrive at any moment, her suspicion lurking like a tightening noose. Her probing questions, the doubts she'd raised about his and Adam's past in Ohio, clawed their way back into his mind. He had sensed a shift in her. She had pulled away from him, not sharing her theories of the case and had assigned the grunt work of tracking down the club's financials. It was out of character. Even the way she had reacted to his request to pick him up. No jokes. No teasing.

She was onto him.

Inside the garage, he fixated on the blue tarp covering his old Chevy pickup truck, a reminder of the past, a past he had tried so hard to bury. A sudden rumble of an engine sent a jolt of fear through him. Peering through a small window, he spotted Lexi's black SUV pulling into the driveway. Two impatient honks pierced the air. He ignored the frantic plea. Minutes later, she sprinted in the rain to the front door and knocked. He could see the confusion in her blue eyes. When he didn't answer, she pulled out her cell phone.

His phone was clutched in his hand, powered off

preemptively to ensure his presence at the house remained hidden. His breath quickened, and he calculated his next move.

Every muscle in his body stiffened as he watched her try to peer into the windows. Once she left, he would concoct a false narrative, a text about catching a ride with another agent. Adam didn't deserve her. He had witnessed firsthand the devastation Adam had caused to their family, and he wouldn't allow him to ruin Lexi's life like he had Victoria's.

#

Thunder cracked, and rain hammered against the roof of the SUV. Lexi cranked the wipers on high and squinted through the window at the deluge of water on the road. Approaching the warehouse located in a commercial strip in the east end, she was distracted by questions about Jake's whereabouts. Why hadn't he been home? The unanswered calls and four text messages fueled her fear. At the back of the warehouse, a faded white sign with black letters that read "Horizon Storage" hung above the door. Her cell phone pinged, and she snatched the device from the passenger seat.

Hey, sorry. I grabbed a ride with Steve Michaels. Catch up with you after the meeting.

Suspicion prickled. It wasn't just the sudden change in Jake's plans; it was the silence before his message. Headlights in the rearview mirror caught her attention. Lexi twisted in the seat and watched Nick's vehicle roll to a stop next to hers. The engine shut off, and the window rolled down.

Lexi lowered her window. Cold rain sprayed her face. "Did you get the search warrant?"

He waved the document like it was a prize. "The place looks abandoned."

She nodded and grabbed the flashlight from the glove box, her heart pounding wildly as Nick retrieved the bolt cutters from his truck. Stepping out of the vehicle, Lexi pulled her coat's hood snug over her head. Rain pounded against the metal roof of the building, sounding like a tin drum. Lightning briefly illuminated the structure, and she followed Nick to the door, gripping her gun and flashlight. He snapped the padlock with a loud crack then pulled out his weapon.

Inside, the air was thick with the smell of wood and dust. Lexi's flashlight punctured the darkness, revealing a twenty-foot boat with an outboard motor. They looked at each other.

"Son of a bitch. You were right about Ryder."

She felt her throat close up and for a few seconds she found it difficult to breathe. "We need the Evidence Response Team here now."

Nick fished the cell phone from his coat pocket and made the call.

A roll of rope lay haphazardly nearby, identical to what had bound the victims to the crosses. Farther ahead, neatly stacked wood planks sent a cold shiver through her veins. The wood matched the crosses found at the crime scenes. A large opened cardboard box held a dozen orange flotation devices.

"They're on the way," Nick said, his gaze sweeping the scene. "Jesus. He constructed the crosses right here. Welcome to the devil's workshop. He played all of us."

"I can't believe I didn't see it sooner." A gas generator, an electric saw, and various tools only cemented her fear. The evidence screamed of premeditation, and the realization hit home that she had been living a lie. Lexi had never suspected the horrors Jake was capable of. He hadn't uttered a word of truth in all the time she had known him.

Venturing deeper into the large space, their steps thumped against the dirty cement floor. She stopped abruptly, her flashlight revealing a wall covered with red-painted words.

"Looks like a bible verse or something," Nick said, squinting.

Lexi read it out loud. "Fracture for fracture, eye for eye, tooth for tooth. The injury inflicted must be suffered in return." Her knees weakened, and she gasped. "Oh, my God. He's going after Adam."

#

Less than five minutes away from their home, Lexi slammed the gas pedal to the floor. The engine growled, and the vehicle fishtailed around the rain-slick corner. The thought of losing Adam to Jake's madness was unbearable. With each unanswered call, her desperation deepened. After leaving another frantic message, Lexi shut off the flashing lights and parked discreetly, a block away from the house. Bolting out of the vehicle, she sprinted down the sidewalk to the front door. Her hands shook so much she struggled to insert the key into the lock. Finally managing to unlock the door, she cautiously entered, two-handing her gun.

The house was too quiet.

After searching every room on the main floor, she descended to the rec room. Finding nothing, panic surged. She dialed Adam again, praying for a miracle. "Pick up, dammit."

Ringing echoed through the house. Hope flickered when she heard his ringtone coming from the upstairs bedrooms. Racing up the staircase, she burst into the master bedroom.

Time stood still.

The dresser lay overturned, and the smoked glass table lamp was smashed. Lexi spotted a large bright red splotch of blood on the gray carpet. She cautiously went to the closet with her gun drawn. Easing it open, she found it empty. Emotions spiraled from disbelief to paralyzing fear. She was too late. Jake had Adam.

Her phone buzzed, Nick's name glaring on the display. She answered, struggling to speak. "Adam's not here. Blood—signs of a struggle—Jake has him."

"Stay calm. Don't touch anything. I'm on my way."

Fear threatened to overwhelm her. She couldn't wait for Nick to arrive. As she ran back to the main floor, it hit her. Jake would take Adam to where it all began: Alum Creek Lake, Ohio. The destination was clear. The means of transport, a mystery. Had he rented a car? Time was against her, a six to seven-hour drive standing between her and Adam. She had to reach Alum Creek Lake before it was too late.

#

The rhythmic thumping of the helicopter's rotor blades reverberated through her body, and memories of Adam flooded her mind, his smile, his laughter. Lexi refused to let him become another victim. His voice echoed in her head, urging her on, bolstering her resolve. Secured in the harness, she leaned against the window, raindrops distorting her view of Alum Creek State Park below.

The pilot's voice broke through her thoughts. "ETA ten minutes. Weather conditions remain unfavorable."

Along the lake's edge, dark trees framed the water, resembling an abstract painting through the rain-smeared glass. They'd been airborne for nearly three hours. Thanks to her SAC's swift action in securing one of the Bureau's helicopters, she would arrive a couple of hours ahead of Jake, providing a critical advantage.

Her phone buzzed.

Nick hissed with frustration in her ear. "Where the hell are you?"

"I'm in Ohio, aboard a chopper, over Alum Creek State Park."

"Tell me you're kidding. I thought I made myself clear. You were supposed to wait for me at the house."

"There was no time to spare. I have to find Adam."

"Going after Jake alone? Without backup? Lexi, dammit. This isn't a solo mission. You're risking your life."

His words were like a cement block sitting on her chest. "I need to find him."

"Not alone, you're not. Don't be reckless."

"I have to go. We're landing soon."

"Wait. I'll alert the local authorities to back you up."

"No, don't. If Jake suspects something's off, he'll kill Adam. Let me handle this my way. Please."

A tense pause, then Nick's tone softened. "Watch your back. Call me as soon as you have him in custody."

"Preparing for descent," the pilot announced.

"I have to go." Her fingers tightened around the seat's edges. She released the harness and removed her headset, grateful to be on solid ground. The side door slid open. Lexi dashed toward a waiting vehicle. Wind whipped through her hair, and rain stung her face. She couldn't shake the fear that she might be too late to save Adam. Yanking the vehicle's door open, she slid onto the passenger seat.

The man behind the wheel ran a hand through his silver-flecked hair. "Lexi Stone? I'm Matt Ryder, Jake's father."

CHAPTER NINE

Lexi followed Matt into his cabin, the oak floor creaking beneath her boots. His attire was simple: jeans and a thick red and black flannel shirt. Blue eyes, deep and contemplative, betrayed the weight of a father's concern for his son's actions. She settled into a seat across from him at a round wooden table, its surface scratched from years of use. Photographs lined one wall, frozen moments in time at the lake, featuring a younger Jake with a proud smile, holding up a large fish.

"Jake's reliving the past," Lexi said.

An uneasy silence enveloped them.

"I doubt he'll listen to me. I lost my son a long time ago." Bitterness tainted his voice. "We've been estranged since the day Victoria died."

"Jake made it sound like you two have been in touch regularly."

He shook his head. "I wish that were true."

The revelation shook Lexi to the core. Every word her partner had spoken felt like a betrayal. Anger bubbled within her, threatening to overflow.

"What's the evidence look like? You said he killed four women when you called. You know, a cop never truly retires."

Her thoughts remained consumed by the shock of discovering the extent of Jake's deception. "It's compelling." She laid out the grisly facts.

He let out a heavy breath. " thought people could change, but sometimes the darkness runs too deep. Never imagined my own son would become a serial killer."

"None of us could have foreseen this." She noticed an old fishing rod leaning against the wall. A few lures hung from it, catching the light from a lamp. "Tell me about Jake. What was he like growing up?"

"He had a fire in him to serve and protect at a young age. Victoria's death destroyed him, pulverized all of us, and changed him. It was like the light inside him went out. He was never one to open up about his feelings. There was a time when he used to love spending hours down at the lake, fishing mostly. It was his escape from everything. The darkness I mentioned settled in after his sister died. I tried to reach out, to help him cope. He shut me out."

Lexi's mind raced with questions and her training kicked in. "Had he ever shown signs of violence before?"

"Only once I'm aware of. When he was seventeen, he dated a girl, Sarah. Their relationship was tumultuous, marked by constant arguments and jealousy. One night he was drinking, he lost control, and left some nasty bruises on her arms. They broke up. No charges were filed."

Every piece of information cemented the profile

she'd constructed. She looked around the cabin and noticed the absence of any feminine touch. "What about his mother? Is she still around?"

"Unfortunately, we divorced after Victoria's death. Joan couldn't stay here. It was too much for her. She moved to Arizona."

"I'm sorry. I know this is difficult for you, but I need your help to bring Jake in. I can't lose Adam."

His eyes reflected the struggle of a man torn between justice and love for his son.

"Jake and Adam were best friends for a long time. I never blamed Adam for Victoria's death. They were kids, and breakups happen. Eric Pittman killed my daughter. He's the one to blame. Adam is a good guy. I always liked him."

Lexi spoke softly. "I know you've lost Jake in more ways than one. If there's a chance we can reach him, we have to try. He'll be here soon."

A heavy silence hung in the air, and then Matt's gaze locked with hers. "I'll help you."

#

Two hundred yards from the water's edge, amid the dense underbrush where the stony shore met the lake's dark depths, Lexi crouched next to Matt feet away. The lake's surface rippled from the cold rain streaming down, soaking them to the bone. Beneath her coat, she felt the weight of her bulletproof vest, a reminder of the danger they faced. It was difficult for her to fathom the agony Matt must be going through, returning to the place where he had found his daughter's body.

"I never thought I'd end up here again," Matt whispered, his voice heavy with the torment of a father forced to confront the past.

Her grip secured around the handle of her weapon. "We have to end this. There isn't any other choice."

A deafening thunderclap shook the ground, followed by a brilliant flash of lightning. From the shadows Jake emerged, his tall figure moving swiftly into the open. With a surge of violent emotion, he shoved Adam hard ahead of him. Adam's face winced in pain.

"This is where Victoria died. Take a good look. My father found her in this exact spot. And this is where you are going to die. If it weren't for you, she'd still be alive. You killed her," Jake yelled.

Lexi felt a sinking feeling in her chest at the sight of Adam, battered and bound. Both eyes were swollen, barely open, and bruised. Jake had completely lost his mind. He was insane. She exchanged a glance with Matt, knowing this was their only chance to resolve the situation without further bloodshed.

She jumped to her feet, every sense heightened. "It's over, Jake. Get on the ground. Hands behind your head. I promise I'll find a way to help you."

Matt stood up beside her, his Smith & Wesson aimed at Jake, his hand trembling slightly. "Son, let him go."

"Dad?" Jake's eyes widened in surprise. "You shouldn't be here. This has nothing to do with you."

"You're my son. It has everything to do with me."

Jake's gaze shifted to Lexi. "I did this for you. He killed Victoria and destroyed our family. I couldn't watch him ruin your life too. He doesn't deserve you."

Each raindrop felt like an icy stab against her face. "Adam had nothing to do with Victoria's death. You know that. Let him go. Do it for me, Jake. Please."

"If I don't? What are you going to do, shoot me?"

Please don't make me do this. She glanced at Adam and felt his fear. "I'm not asking you again."

"Jake, please," Matt begged. "We don't want anyone else to get hurt. I love you. You're still my son. Let's find another way out of this."

Jake stood there and just looked at them for a long moment. His hand twitched. A glint of metal caught Lexi's eye.

A sharp crack. A gunshot splintered the air with deadly precision.

Adam crumpled to the ground.

"No!" *This isn't how it's supposed to end.* Tears blurred Lexi's vision. Her legs felt like lead as she rushed forward, her focus locked on Adam.

Matt fired another shot.

The bullet tore into Jake's right leg. His face contorted in pain. He stumbled sideways and almost lost his balance, but he managed to get off a round.

Hot pain seared Lexi's right forearm. She flinched and felt warm blood travel down her hand. Her weapon felt heavier with every passing second. Struggling to hold it steady, she locked eyes with Matt.

"I'm so sorry, son." Matt fired again.

The shot struck Jake squarely in the chest, sending him sprawling backward into the wet sand.

#

Lexi pushed open the door to Adam's room in the intensive care unit at Grady Memorial Hospital. The smell of strong antiseptic assaulted her nostrils. Adam lay motionless, a network of tubes and wires surrounding him, his face pale under the harsh glare of the fluorescent lights. The steady hum of medical equipment merged with the insistent beeps from multiple monitors stationed around his bed.

The bullet had entered his left side, just below his rib cage, causing extensive damage to his internal organs. Even after emergency surgery, the odds were stacked against him. Guilt whispered at her, and Lexi wished she could turn back time. She reached to touch his hand but hesitated, fearing any disturbance might disrupt the fragile balance keeping him alive.

Nick's arrival disrupted her thoughts, the soles of his shoes squeaking on the polished white linoleum floor. "How's he doing?"

Her injured arm throbbed. She pushed the discomfort aside. It was nothing compared to the agony of seeing Adam like this. She shook her head. "Hanging on."

"He's tough. He's going to pull through."

The worst-case scenario played in her mind, and her voice strained. "What if he doesn't?"

He didn't answer.

A male nurse with a composed demeanor and close-cropped hair approached the bed, his gaze sweeping the monitors with practiced efficiency. "The doctors are doing everything they can. He's a fighter."

Lexi managed a weak smile, grateful for any glimmer of hope, and glanced at Adam. His eyelids remained closed, the only sign of life the steady rise and fall of his chest.

"Matt Ryder's been cleared. The shooting's been deemed self-defense," Nick said after the nurse left the room. "He's in the morgue with Jake."

The mention of Matt and the sacrifice he made to save them momentarily diverted her thoughts. She pictured him standing over Jake's body, grappling with his decision. She couldn't dwell on it now. Her focus had to be on Adam.

Suddenly, the heart monitors let out a frantic series of beeps.

Panic tore through her.

Nurses and doctors flooded into the room, a whirlwind of white coats swirling past her.

"Code Blue!" someone shouted.

Tubes and wires were hastily unplugged.

"We're losing him!" a nurse cried out.

Another nurse began chest compressions.

She felt Nick's hand on her arm. "Adam, you can't leave me now. I love you."

"Clear the room!" a determined female doctor ordered.

A male nurse ushered her and Nick out of the

room. Lexi thought of all the words left unsaid, the promises of a future, their dreams destroyed in an instant.

The defibrillator delivered a powerful jolt of electricity, causing Adam's body to convulse.

"One milligram of epinephrine, now," the doctor shouted.

The nurse administered the drug. Seconds felt like an eternity. Then he shook his head.

"Again," the doctor said. "Clear!" Another shock surged through Adam's body. "One more milligram of epinephrine."

Tears blurred Lexi's vision, and her heart stuck in her throat. She silently pleaded they'd be able to save the man she couldn't bear to lose.

Finally, a faint blip of green appeared on the monitor, and the alarms ceased.

The doctor stepped back. "We've got sinus rhythm. He's stable for now."

Lexi dashed back into the room.

Adam's eyelids fluttered open. "Lexi..."

She grasped his hand, her eyes never leaving his face. "I'm here. I'm not going anywhere."

CHAPTER TEN

Two months later...

Past events played over in Lexi's mind, a slideshow of pain and regret. Adam's recovery had been agonizingly slow, nearly a month confined in the hospital, his body healing slower than his spirit. She was grateful he had survived, but the physical and emotional scars would remain with him forever. Matt had retreated into a world of grief and guilt. He had become a shell of the man he once was, haunted by the impossible decision he had been forced to make. His son, gone. The price of justice. Jake's name would forever be a dark stain on the city. He was the one who had called in the anonymous tip about the call girl service and set up Adam to take the fall for the murders in every way possible. He had left behind a trail of shattered lives, unanswered questions, and a community struggling to make sense of the senseless. But there was a glimmer of hope. Love had prevailed.

Outside the weathered stone walls of the Traverse City Winery, the sun dipped below the horizon, casting a golden hue over the sprawling snow-covered vineyard. Lexi clutched a bouquet of red roses, her breath forming wispy clouds in the crisp January air. Beside her, a ten-foot outdoor heater hummed with warmth.

Her father kissed her forehead. "I love you, kid. You deserve every happiness in the world. I couldn't be prouder."

Blinking back tears, she fought against the surge of emotion. "Dad, you're gonna mess up my makeup." Adjusting the hem of her tea-length white lace gown and pulling the faux fur-trimmed cape around her shoulders, she glanced at Adam at the altar in a sleek black wool suit. His smile captured her heart, just as it had when they first met.

While *"A Thousand Years"* by Christina Perri played from the outdoor speakers, Lexi walked arm in arm with her father to the altar. She stopped, and he took a seat in the front row next to her mother. Lexi noticed her mother dabbing her eyes with a tissue. This could be a turning point. The gap between them seemed insurmountable, years of missed opportunities to truly bond. Her thoughts drifted to Jake, his betrayal a festering wound. Time to forgive, to let go. She deserved a second chance at happiness.

"You look breathtaking," Adam said, his voice soft with admiration.

Fairy lights draped over nearby trees and cast a gentle radiance on his face. "So do you. Are you ready for this?"

He flashed a grin. "More than you can imagine."

Wearing a well-fitted charcoal suit, the officiant, Ethan, a friend of a colleague from the Bureau, began the ceremony. "We are gathered here today to celebrate the love between Lexi and Adam." He gave them a nod.

A loud clatter made Lexi's heart skip a beat. Her gaze darted toward the commotion. A male guest talking on his cell phone had accidentally knocked over a stack of champagne glasses, prompting a few nervous chuckles and a brief pause in the proceedings. He looked vaguely familiar, but she couldn't place him.

She refocused on Adam.

He took a long breath and let it out. "I, Adam, take you, Lexi, to be my lawfully wedded wife. Three years ago, we found each other. Your presence and energy are magnetic. You are, and always have been, exactly what I need in my life; a partner, lover, friend, the one person I can always rely on."

"Adam, your easygoing nature and kindness is what drew me in, and I found someone who never pushed and always understood." Lexi inhaled a steadying breath. "You were, and still are, the one person I love and trust. You are my everything."

Adam's eyes shone.

Ethan continued. "May I have the rings, please?"

Her father stood and passed them to him.

Adam slipped the white gold band onto her finger, his touch tender and loving. "With this ring, I seal my love for you."

Lexi slid a matching wedding ring onto his finger. "With this ring, I pledge my heart forever."

"By the power vested in me, I now pronounce you husband and wife. You may kiss the bride."

Her lips met Adam's, and applause erupted from their forty guests. He took her hand, and they walked back up the aisle toward the indoor reception.

Lexi peered through the window at the string lights crisscrossing the ceiling and the tables draped in white cloths with centerpieces of red roses and flickering candles. "We did it."

He kissed her hand. "We sure did, Lexi Quinn."

Her gaze briefly landed on David Williams and his wife, and then onto Nick. He had finally moved on, dating the same woman, a schoolteacher, for over a month. Lexi was happy for him.

Cell phones suddenly went off.

"Not now." Adam frowned and dug his phone out of his suit pocket.

"We haven't even had the first dance." Lexi sighed and reached for her device buried within her bouquet. She felt the blood drain from her face at the single word message. "Kaboom!" Then she saw the man who had broken the champagne glasses, walking toward her. *Lucas Turner...the kidnapping case six years ago...*

Their eyes locked, and she knew.

"I want you to feel what it's like to lose everything you care about!"

Panic clawed her throat. "Everyone, get out of the

building!" Her grip slipped from Adam's hand.

Bodies blurred by.

A flash of white light blinded her, followed by a deafening bang.

Lexi was slammed onto the ceramic floor. Bones cracked. The world seemed to tilt on its axis.

Her ears rang with a cacophony of screams, drowning out all rational thought. Shards of glass rained down like lethal confetti, slicing through flesh and bone. Her breath came out in short, ragged gasps and she felt the wetness of blood pool beneath her. Metal beams overhead suddenly groaned like angry beasts and snapped. The roof creaked, then collapsed, engulfing everything in a cloud of debris.

Lexi reached and called out, her voice hoarse and desperate. "Adam!"

He wasn't there.

Distant cries of pain and anguish echoed through the smoke-choked air. As she struggled to regain her bearings, Lexi tried to move, but something was on top of her. She let out a silent scream. In an adrenaline-fueled frenzy, she shoved Nick's lifeless form aside, climbed to one knee, then the other, and stumbled forward, her wedding dress like a vise around her legs, impeding her movement.

Amid the choking haze, twisted and bloodied bodies of their guests were strewn throughout the carnage. She spotted her parents, mangled and motionless, trapped beneath the steel beams. It was all too much to process, too surreal to be real. Lexi staggered, her vision fading in and out. Ahead, a hand reached out deep from the rubble. Snow swirled around her, and the world spun and swayed. Then everything descended into darkness.

AUTHOR NOTE

I hope you've enjoyed reading All the Bad Girls. Please be sure to leave review!

To my fans, readers, reviews--thank you!
You rock!

Love reading heart-pounding thrillers? Don't forget to check out all of Kim's other books.

Want to learn more about Kim and her books?
Visit www.kimcresswell.ca

ABOUT THE AUTHOR

Kim Cresswell

resides in Ontario, Canada, and is the award-winning author of the action-packed Whitney Steel romantic suspense series. As a multi-genre author, her books have been featured online at USA Today, NBC, FOX, Publishers Weekly, Booklife, and ScifiPulse.net. The Assassin Chronicles TV series was in development with Council Tree Productions. The TV series is based on Kim's paranormal suspense thriller, Deadly Shadow, and the highly anticipated sequel, Invisible Truth.

BOOKS BY KIM CRESSWELL

Whitney Steel Series
Reflection (Book One)
Retribution (Book Two)
Resurrect (Book Three)

The Assassin Chronicles
Deadly Shadow (Book One)

The Sum of all Tears
Icehaven (Book One)
Liberty (Book Two)

The Raina Storm Series
Dawn of the Storm (Book One)
Dawn of the Enemy (Book Two)

Novellas
All the Bad Girls
Hell's Bounty Hunter
Seeking Hope

Lethal Journey

True Crime Short Stories
Real Life Evil
Murder on Sunset Strip
Garden of Bones
Edge of Madness
Chameleon
Backwoods Murder

True Crime Anthologies Published
by Grinning Man Press
Serial Killer Quarterly, "21st Century Psychos"
Serial Killer Quarterly, "Partners in Pain"
Serial Killer Quarterly, "Unsolved in North America"
Serial Killer Quarterly, "Cruel Britannia"
Serial Killer Quarterly, "They Almost Got Away"
Serial Killer Quarterly, "Lostmord:
Murder in German"